Time Traveller

JO Meets *Shakespeare*

Time Traveller

JO Meets
Shakespeare

Sarah Garrett & Morag Ramsay

Seven Arches
Publishing

Published in 2013
By Seven Arches Publishing
27, Church Street, Nassington, Peterborough PE8 61QG
www.sevenarchespublishing.co.uk

A catalogue record for this book is available from the British Library.

Design, scans and typesetting by Alan McGlynn.
Cover Illustration by John Bigwood.

Printed in Great Britain.

ISBN 978-0-9567572-3-4

‹IF THIS IS THE FIRST TIME YOU HAVE READ ONE OF THE BOOKS THAT RECORDS THE ADVENTURES OF CHILDREN FROM THE TWENTY FIRST CENTURY IN A TIMEZONE DIFFERENT TO TODAY, YOU NEED TO KNOW›

›   That SHARP stands for The Scientific History and Art Reclamation Programme.

›   That STRAP stands for the Scientific Testing and Recording of Aggression Programme.

›   That time slip is something that you might suffer if you travel through time and space, in a similar way to how some people get jet lag when they fly long distances on a jet air liner.

›   That if you travel through time and space you are a xrosmonaut.

CHAPTER 1

A School Trip From Oxford To The Globe, Bankside, London

'I don't know why I chose to sit next to you on this trip, Jo,' said Ruby as the school coach, packed with Year 8s, turned off the M4 into the traffic-clogged streets of West London.

'Mmm,' came the reply from Jo, staring intensely out of the window as if there were some possibility of spotting Justin Bieber on a Hammersmith street corner.

'It wasn't just because you're my best friend, well that was one reason, but not the main one…' The tone in Ruby's voice became sarcastic, 'no, my main reason was because I knew you would be the person most likely to help me pass a boring couple of hours – that you'd be fun, fun, fun all the way.'

'Mmm… mm?' Came from Jo again; this time a little more drawn out and with the possibility of a question mark at the end.

'Scintillating conversation, jokes and wisecracks, sharing unbelievable gossip; I mean it's been a laugh a minute all the way from Oxford. Not.' The 'not' came out loudly, so loudly that Jo gave a small jump as if suddenly realising where she was. She made a big effort to turn towards her friend, leaving the London streets to slowly grind past without her attention.

'I'm really sorry, Ruby. I know I've been no fun. You should have sat with Emily.'

'You can say that again,' Ruby said bluntly. But then, after an awkward pause, she added more kindly: 'Is everything alright? I mean are you worried about something, Jo? It's like I've been sitting next to a zombie all the way from school.'

'I've had a lot on my mind just recently.'

'You're not still upset about Stuart are you?'

'No. I've never been upset about him.' Jo blushed as she said this.

'Oh that's a whopper! You know I don't believe that!'

'Well, alright, I was upset to start with. We got on so well when he first joined the band. And, yes I did think he liked me, but that wasn't what mattered. He was a real asset to the band and he made a difference. When it was just me on drums, you on keyboard and Emily singing, we were a bit thin. Then when Stuart joined us with guitar, our sound was much stronger.

And we all had a lot of fun – didn't we?'

'Yeah, true, absolutely.'

'And then Stuart and Emily start getting all 'lovesy-dovesy'. It changed things – you felt it as well, I know you did.'

'Of course I did. But I'm not the one wasting a lot of time worrying about it. So what do you want to do? Break up the band? Is that what you've been stressing over?'

'Sort of,' Jo lied and turned back to face the window. She hated lying to Ruby, to anyone else it was easy, but not to Ruby; she was such a good friend, a million times more reliable than the once-best-friend Emily. But the thoughts that had been filling her mind were ones she couldn't share with anyone. Well, no one except a strange girl who lived in a future time and who, after almost six months of not contacting her, had decided to get in touch that morning. Just as she had been putting her sandwiches into her backpack, her BlackBerry had buzzed with the special tone that told her that Mela, the girl from the future, was contacting her. Mela left a cryptic message that said she would be back in touch later that day. Nothing more! What was the use of that? Jo had felt so cross, but all she could do was press the reply button and that never resulted in

Mela getting back. Now she had to spend the day worrying that she might not be able to answer a message from the person she had been longing to speak to for months. School trips were not good for taking private messages; there was always someone peering over your phone, or getting annoyed if you didn't share.

'Jo… you can't just say you're thinking of breaking up the band and leave it hanging in the air. I'm part of this band as well you know.' There was a splutter of anger in Ruby's voice. Then, to Jo's great relief, Ruby's phone went. Ruby pulled her iPhone out of her bag, while Jo's fingers tightened around her Black-Berry.

'Oh! Fantastic !' Ruby's face lit up like an award winning actress accepting a Bafta. 'Oh fabulous! My Aunt Sharma has sent me pictures of the wedding!' Suddenly all was excitement. Ruby had only got back from Kerala in India a few days before. She, her mum and dad plus her small brother had joined a huge contingent of relatives for the wedding of one of Ruby's cousins. It had been one of the most wonderful weeks of her life, Ruby had told them all about twenty times.

Delightedly, Ruby started showing Jo the colourful pictures of a wedding in India. Jo 'oohed' and 'aahed' appropriately. As Ruby relived her memories of the 'best week of her life', she didn't notice that, after a while, Jo had turned to stare out of the window once again as the coach neared its destination: the South Bank of the Thames where, once, in 1599, someone called William Shakespeare had joined with others to commission the building of a theatre called the Globe. Like all the other students who had arrived in coaches from many different schools across the country, Jo and her friends from Oxford' s High School for Girls clambered off their coach, stretched their legs and joined the queue at the entrance of a new Globe theatre. They had tickets for a guided tour in the morning and a performance in the afternoon.

'Now, settle down everyone, please. I know there is lots to see and some of you have started to unwrap your sandwiches. Just forget about food for a moment now…and boys too. Yes, I can see where your eyes are going.' Miss Marshal, their head of year, gave a grin. 'I quite agree there are some gorgeous hunks about, but our time here at the Globe is short. Tell me, did you enjoy the theatre tour this morning?'

There were enthusiastic replies of: 'Fantastic', 'Absolutely great', 'I learnt such a lot'.

'I did too and thank you all for behaving so well.

Now that we can see it from the outside, having been round the interior, we can appreciate what an amazing building it is. It is a truly inspiring example of historical research, isn't it?' the teacher paused.

'Yes, Miss Marshal,' the girls all riveted their eyes on the young, popular teacher in front of them. They were sitting on picnic benches on the open space leading down to the river in the area called Bankside. Wonderful, warm, late June sunshine was already attacking the sun block they had all applied to the back of their necks and their arms.

'But, you tell me: what are the reasons that make it so inspiring?' asked Miss Marshal. Hands shot up. They were bright, well-taught girls… and they had all been on the internet. They tried to put into words the passion of the American actor/director Sam Wanamaker. They knew it had taken him twenty years to realise his dream of recreating Shakespeare's Globe theatre. They knew a lot of other things as well: that it was built using the building methods of the tradesmen who had built the original Globe; that it was not round, but a many-sided polygon; that it was like a doughnut with an outer covered ring and the inside a space open to the elements. They knew that the roof was built of thatch.

'What is so special about that?' asked Miss Marshal, her eyebrows arched questioningly, knowing she had probably hit a spot that would stretch their thinking a little further.

'Is it because the original Globe caught on fire because it had a thatched roof?' a studious girl called Susie responded.

'An excellent answer, Susie, but not quite what I was looking for. Anyone want to try another answer?'

The girls were silent.

'Well, what happened to London in 1666?'

Nearly every hand shot up: 'The Great Fire of London,' they almost shouted, which earned an envious glance from a teacher with another group of not so attentive students sitting nearby.

'Exactly. The thatched roof over the new Globe is the first thatched roof ever to be permitted in London since the Fire.'

'Did they have to have a special Act of Parliament to build it?' asked Susie.

'Do you know, I don't know the answer to that, Susie. You might be able to ask someone at the Globe later today.' Miss Marshal looked down at her phone to check the time. 'We must get on with our lunch now, or we'll be late for the performance. You can unwrap your sandwiches, girls.'

Usually very sociable, Jo was glad to be sitting on the edge of the group and to see that Ruby was excitedly showing her wedding pictures to Emily and two other girls. She didn't want anyone to talk to her, so she concentrated hard on the sandwiches in her lunch box. But if asked what she was eating, she wouldn't have been able to say. She felt so strange, other worldly, from a different time and space to all these chattering girls around her.

There was no doubt about it – time travel changed you. Her first adventure was six months ago. For all those months, she had been unable to tell anyone that she had actually met two of the most famous writers of the twentieth century, both long dead before she was born. Jo had gone back to 1940 and met the two greatest writers of the period, Tolkien and C. S. Lewis at their lodgings in Oxford University. Somehow, during the months that followed, it had seemed easy keeping this wonderful adventure secret; but suddenly, she was finding it almost impossible to stifle the urge to tell someone. She wanted to stand up and go and say to Miss Marshal, 'Do you realise, I've talked with Tolkein and C. S. Lewis?' Fortunately, she knew all too well what a disaster that would be. But why was she even thinking of such a thing? Why, why did she feel so jittery? It could only mean they, the organisation from the future, were going to send her back in time again – that's why they had got in touch with her this morning. Jo got up and went to stand near her teacher.

'Yes, Jo what is it?' Miss Marshal looked up and smiled at one of her favourite pupils, not the cleverest girl in the class, nor the most talented, but certainly the kindest and most creative.

'Will we be able to see the spot where the original Globe stood?' Jo asked. She wanted to know the answer because when they had all gone to the toilets after getting off the coach, she had received another message from Mela. It had simply said: 'Make sure to visit the site of the original Globe'.

'Oh, thank you for reminding me of that, Jo. Though there's not much to see – there's just a plaque on a wall just a short distance, maybe a couple of hundred yards from the present-day Globe but yes, we will go to see it before we get back on the coach. First of all though, we have this wonderful opportunity, part of this marvelous Literary Olympiad, of seeing a German company perform 'A Midsummer's Night's Dream' – I'm so looking forward to it. But don't let me forget about the plaque.'

CHAPTER 2

A School Trip From Edinburgh To The Globe, Bankside, London

'Honestly Alex, I think you're old enough now to make sure you've got enough clean clothes for three days down in London!' Maureen, Alex's mum was stooping down in front of the washing machine, pulling out handfuls of Alex's under-pants and T-shirts and swiftly transferring them to the drier. 'Doing emergency washing and drying for a son, who's taller than I am, is not what I had in mind for my day off!'

'But Mum, I've got enough clothes packed already, honestly, I have. And anyway, Dad said he'd put that extra load on for me this morning but he for...' Alex never got to finish. Jock, his father, had just got back from work and was clattering up the stairs and through the open door of their cramped flat.

'I heard that, son. Ye'er no' laying the blame on me. I've been stacking shelves for five days and I haven't a muscle that disnae ache.' Jock leaned towards Maureen and gave her a quick peck on the cheek as she straightened up from in front of the washer.

'Here's a tenner son – fast forward to the chippy and get the usual. You'll have just enough time to woof it down before you have tae catch that night coach from St. Andrew Square. Are you packed?'

'He's almost done and I'm adding a few extra items so he's not going round London in the same smelly T-shirt for three days.' Maureen got in.

Alex grinned at his dad, who had shot him a raised-eye-brow-trust-women-to-fuss look.

'Thanks,' Alex grabbed the tenner. 'Good idea Dad – I'm off to the chippy now.'

The door banged as Alex made a quick getaway. Jock sat down heavily at the kitchen table. He said nothing for a moment or two, but let out a sigh and shook his head, his shoulders hunched.

'Stop fretting, Jock. You're doing your best.'

'Aye, but it's nae good enough, is it? If I had my old job back...' He tailed off without finishing the words that had been said many times before. The sigh came again. 'All I can say is it's a good job we've only the one kiddie.'

'Exactly, and we can afford to give him what he needs. Not all the lads and lassies in his class are going on this trip. I know for a fact that the Kirkpatrick's boy won't be going.'

'I'd have liked to have given him more than twenty to take with him.'

'Jock, it says on the letter, no more than twenty-five pounds.' Maureen shook a letter with the school crest at the top in front of Jock. 'You gave him twenty and I gave him five, so he's fine'.

Alex's class was to travel down from Edinburgh to London on the overnight coach to visit, amongst other historic sites, the Globe Theatre on the South Bank of the Thames. They would be arriving at 8.00a.m. at Victoria, thus saving them the cost of a hostel for that night.

The small family walked the mile from their home, past the castle, along Princes Street, up St Andrew Street and found the coach tucked away around a corner. Alex was almost the last to be checked in but his mate, Alistair, had got there first and bagged a good seat near the front for them both. Parental goodbyes rippled through the coach like a wave. The boys grinned at each other...

'Did you remember to bring – snap!!' Two mobiles, loaded with games, clinked sides.

Alex was still wide awake at midnight. Alistair,

though, was fast asleep. His head had flopped down on to Alex's shoulder and a rhythmic snortling sound was coming from somewhere deep within his respiratory tract. Alex gave him a shove. No response. The head slipped further down and the snoring continued. Alex gave him another shove, more determined this time.

'What...what? Errr...humph...errr.' Without waking up, Alistair flailed out his arms, and turned over, his face now pressed against the blackened window of their coach, which was steadily thrumming its way down the A1. For a while, Alex thought he had won a respite because, although Alistair was now curled into a ball and his bum was encroaching well and truly into Alex's space, the snoring had stopped.

Sleep began to curl around the edges of his mind, but each time it was about to claim him, the contents of the email he had printed up and put in his jacket pocket would shake him awake, itching him to read it one more time. It was from his girlfriend Ruth, who had moved to San Francisco with her family. It went on and on about how she loved it there and the only bit about him was at the end: 'I'm missing climbing with you at the club and missing you, love Ruth xx' Why two x's and not three? Why small x's and not big ones? She'd written about missing their climbing club almost as much as missing him. True, they had met at the Edinburgh climbing club and were both mad keen on climbing; they'd both made it into the club's junior team. But now, she'd been gone three weeks and it was clear that he was already a fading memory.

He stared out, the dark road in front pierced by the bright headlights of the coach, and then caught site of a motorway sign: Scotch Corner 25 miles. His mobile rang and he jerked wide awake. It was Danny! He had met Danny through the very strange circumstances of being an agent for an organisation from the future specialising in time travel. All thoughts of missing Ruth or trying to get to sleep were banished.

'Hi man, what's with?'

'Hi Alex, Sorry to contact you so late but I've just heard from Kaz and he's asked me to pass on a couple of messages.'

'Why didn't he contact me himself?'

'No idea. You know there's no explaining what SHARP decides to do, though I wouldn't put it past them to use me because it's cheaper for them, energy wise.'

'Yeah, maybe. They always seem to be going on about how much energy time travel uses. But you know what, I wonder if they have money. I mean, they never tell us any stuff about what it's like for them, you know, where they live and everything.' Alex shot a quick look round to see if any of the sleeping students might have woken up. But no, there was no one awake to wonder at this strange conversation.

'I know, I know.' Danny went on. 'I often wonder... It's all very well telling us they come from the distant future, but how distant?'

'After the Dark Chaos, obviously, but when was that... or rather when is that going to happen?'

'Well, as far as I can make out, what they keep saying to me is that what we do is preventing the Dark Chaos from ever happening, which sounds like a good thing. Anyway, they want to know if you are willing to take on something for them. It's pretty special by the sounds of things. I think it involves going back to the time of Shakespeare. I'm sorry I can't be more specific.'

'Danny that's so weird, I am at this point in time, travelling on a coach with a lot of sleeping morons – my Year 8 class that is – from Edinburgh to London on a school trip to the Globe Theatre in London.'

'Ah ha – that explains this next message then, I really didn't know what they were going on about. Apparently, the new Globe Theatre is built almost on the spot of the old one. And the second message is: 'If you do take this one on, can you make contact tomorrow at the Globe with a girl coming on a school visit like you. She's coming with a school from Oxford and her name is Jo Kelly'. It looks as if they want you both to spot each other, so that when they send you back to the same place and time, you can work together or something like that. The thing is, Alex, are you up for it?'

'Why me? Not you, Danny?'

There was a spluttering sound at the end of the phone.

'Are you laughing?'

'I am laughing, because I think I'm getting battle fatigue – like those fighter pilots in World War Two. I think I'm in a different time zone more often than in the one I'm supposed to be in. Sooner or later, I'll make a mistake, and I've got my little sister breathing down my neck. She's a pretty smart cookie and she's sure I'm up to something. Keeps saying I'm working for MI5. So Alex, my mate. I need you.'

'I get the picture and I'm very happy to help, seeing the way my life is going at the moment. I could say I need this as much as those boffins at SHARP need me.'

'Great, speak soon. I'll let Kaz know you're up for it. Thanks mate.'

Alex's reply was lost as Danny clicked off. Alex slipped his phone into his backpack, sprawled his legs out into the corridor and promptly fell asleep.

CHAPTER 3

Imagination

The queue to get into the Globe to see the performance of *A Midsummer's Night's Dream* had moved slowly, the excited chatter of teenage voices from school groups drowned out by a heady mix of languages from across the world. Now inside and making their way to the ticket check in, Jo found it difficult to keep up with the others in her school group. The focus of her attention was snatched up by the passing snippets of conversation from the throng of people whose enthusiasm for the reconstructed Globe seemed almost palpable. Miss Marshal's instruction to keep together was getting harder and harder to follow. The teacher had explained that Globe officials would not let anyone into the performance unless the whole school party went in together; ten students to each accompanying adult. Jo was one of the ten attached to Mrs Butler, a mum who had agreed to help out and, right now, Jo could only just glimpse Mrs Butler's left shoulder about three or four people ahead of her. She'd being trying to catch up but two American women, loudly chattering, blocked her way.

Suddenly, a clear and precise voice came into Jo's head. 'Jo this is Mela,' the voice said. 'I'm sorry I've never told you about our thought transference options before, but I haven't needed to until now. Now I've got to give you this message quickly: there's a boy on your right, almost going past you. Their line is moving faster than yours. You've got to be quick.'

Jo's eyes swiveled to the right; a tall, good-looking boy, part of a noisy school group, (who sounded as if they were from Scotland), was moving along in the queue to her right, a step ahead of her.

'Tap on his arm and say: Are you Alex?' came Mela's voice inside her head.

'What?' Jo gasped out loud.

Inside her head, the thought came back to her, loud and insistent. 'Just do it Jo.'

As she wavered uncertainly, the boy got a little further ahead; that queue was definitely moving faster than hers. Jo squeezed to the right and, not caring about being polite anymore, managed to push past the two American women, one telling the other loudly how she wished it was one of the tragedies they were seeing today but... Jo lost track of what followed the 'but', and was now walking almost beside the boy.

She tapped on his arm and he turned to face her – he certainly was an attractive guy.

'Are you Alex?' Jo asked, not bothering to explain herself more fully.

'Jo Kelly!'

It was Jo's turn to feel a shock of surprise. 'How do you know my name?'

'SHARP,' was Alex's one word reply.

Jo nodded. 'SHARP.' Then she giggled. 'This is weird, well weird.'

'It's brilliant,' Alex whispered theatrically. 'It's better than being in MI5. How many times have they sent you back?'

Jo just had time to say, 'twice,' before they reached the ticket barrier. Alex's group was obviously going to go through first and Jo was shepherded into the Oxford group by Mrs Butler. Jo watched as the Globe attendants counted the boys with their teachers through. No chance for them to talk more, but just before Alex disappeared into the theatre space, he turned round and almost shouted, 'Time travelling, time travelling – we're going back in time to 16…'

Everyone smiled and a couple of girls gave an appreciative clap. Jo mischievously said to Mrs Butler: 'That would be brilliant wouldn't it? If we could really go back in time?'

'Well, I'm not sure I would want to swap travelling to London in our nice air-conditioned coach for a seat in a smelly Elizabethan carriage, would you?'

'Mmm, maybe not.'

'And now, we are going to stand for a long time to watch a play. Yes, it will be a little like travelling back in time. We are going to be modern-day 'groundlings'. What a weird name, I suppose it must mean the people who stood on the ground. However, I wouldn't mind seeing the play in a bit of modern-day comfort.'

'Oh, Mrs Butler, you're not getting into the spirit of things.'

'I'm trying to Jo, I am. But I know my feet are going to be aching by the time we get out, and what a good job we all put sun block on, because with no roof over our heads we will catch the sun.'

'Better than it raining, though,' said Jo. 'Just imagine, the groundlings, back in Shakespeare's time paid their penny to stand and watch a play whatever the weather – wind, rain or snow. Just imagine if we were going to the first performance today of *The Dream*.

'Yes, Jo, just imagine as you are saying, but, you

know what my English teacher wrote on my last end of term report? 'Marjorie,' that's me, 'writes competently and clearly but she has NO imagination.''

'Oh that was cruel.'

'No it was true, and it still is.'

By this time they had got into the theatre space and Jo's imagination, if not Mrs Butler's, was working overtime.

The atmosphere of the scene was wrapping itself around her like a magic cloak. She looked up at the balconies, now almost full of adults and families, some of whom had travelled half way across the world to get there. Their faces blurred into a composite picture of an audience. In her mind, they could be Elizabethan lords and ladies. The circle of sky above seemed to add to the magic and when she stood in front the stage with its long, sloping apron coming down towards the groundlings, (the common people), the well-used line 'all the world's a stage' crept into her mind. When the play began, Jo was in another world, a world created by a master of imagination.

When Jo's coach drew up into the grounds of her school in Oxford, amongst the group of adults waiting to collect their children off the bus was her grandma,

Shirley, and her younger brother, Ollie. Her parents, top-flight Oxford academics, were away on a visit to a university in Toronto and Grandma was looking after them.

'How was it, Jo?' Grandma asked as soon as they bundled themselves into her small, bright, yellow runabout.

'Oh, fabulous, Gran just fabulous. *A Midsummer's Night's Dream* was performed by a German group; they have a Globe theatre in Germany. They were excellent.'

Before Gran could ask her any more Ollie, who had been tugging at Jo's arm for attention for a while, spluttered with excitement: 'Grandma's got something to tell you, Jo. It's dead brill!'

'Ollie let's get back home right now. You know I have to concentrate on the road when I'm driving,' said Grandma, as she misjudged the corner out of the school gate and the car bumped over the edge of the pavement. Jo and Ollie gave each other a meaningful glance.

'OK Grandma, you're right. I won't say a thing until we get home,' Ollie said.

Tea was ready to eat the minute they got in and appetising smells coming from the oven were wafting round the house. Jo shot upstairs to go to the toilet and washed her hands. Before she left she felt her phone throbbing. She knew it was Mela but she would have to wait: tea, grandma and Ollie's 'dead brill' news had to come first.

The chicken casserole that Grandma had prepared kept them all quiet for the first part of the meal; Grandma was first in the family stakes for cooking, their mum being too taken up with her numerous academic interests to bother much with the mundane job of feeding her family. But after the first few mouthfuls of the yoghurt they were having for dessert, Ollie prompted Grandma to tell Jo her news.

'As you know, you and Ollie are coming back to Brighton with me in a couple of weeks – at the start of the summer holidays.'

'Mmm…Mum and Dad told us before they went that's what we'd do. Ollie that's not news. It's great, I'm looking forward to it, but it's not news.'

'Shut up and listen,' said Ollie.

'No need to be rude, Ollie. But, yes be a little patient, Jo. You know I have a wide circle of friends in Brighton. In fact, since I moved there I think I have more friends than I've ever had in my life, which is a good job now that your granddad has passed on.'

'Yes, of course it is, Grandma; I'm sure you miss Gramps a lot.'

'Well it's five years now. I miss him but I get on with life and, of course, Brighton is a town where things are always happening.' Grandma paused as she ate a couple of mouthfuls of yoghurt. Then she went on, 'One of my friend's grandchildren is a bit like you Jo, he plays in a fledgling band. It's a boy called... Harry, I think (there seems to be a lot of Harrys around these days). Anyway a month or so ago, he took my friend to this place called, ' The Blind Tiger'. Where do they think up these names?' Another pause and a few more mouthfuls of yoghurt.

'Let me tell Jo, Grandma,' said Ollie, obviously experiencing a lot of impatience himself at Grandma's slow meandering account.

'Yes, you tell her, Ollie'

'The thing is Jo, Grandma has found out that at this place called 'The Blind Tiger', they are going to have afternoon sessions especially for kids, you know teens and stuff and that they are planning to have an open mic session. The people organising it are a group called A-M-I. They're a band, based in Brighton and they seem fantastically popular. Grandma has thought up this idea that your band, Emily, Ruby, Stuart and

26

me as well, of course, could perform at one of these open mic sessions.'

'That sounds fantastic,' butted in Jo, 'but not really possible. How could Emily, Ruby and Stuart come all the way from Oxford for just a session?'

'You under estimate your grandma,' said Ollie, 'she's been busy all day ringing up parents and asking if they can come and stay for a few days.'

'Wow, Grandma!' Jo went round the table and gave her a big hug. 'You are the best grandma ever.'

'Well I would have to be with the best grandchildren in the world.' Their grandma beamed happily at the two of them. 'Now, best grandchildren, you can wash the dishes because I've got to get on with Jo's Elizabethan costume for their play at school. It's almost done, just needs the finishing touches.'

'OMG! It's the play at school tomorrow!' exclaimed Jo. 'Today has been so amazing I completely forgot about the school's Elizabethan pageant. We are supposed to be having an Elizabethan banquet and lucky, lucky Trudi gets to play Elizabeth the first. I hope her mum's good at sewing.'

'Well your costume is more in keeping with a young girl from the merchant class than nobility, but no one will know the difference.'

'Mum would,' said Ollie mischievously.

'Well, she's not here,' said Jo and Grandma in unison.

'And if she wanted perfection, she should have done it herself,' added Grandma.

'She can't sew for toffee,' said Jo, remembering the previous year's fiasco when the school had a Victorian fair and they ended up having to pay a fortune for a costume from a shop in town.

'You don't need to tell me Jo, I think I know why they agreed to this visit to Toronto University for the end of the summer term!'

CHAPTER 4

Serious Stuff

The Elizabethan school pageant was a great success and Jo's costume was a hit. 'Good as any theatrical costume you could hire – good enough for a performance at the Globe,' said Miss Marshal.

Sitting in her costume with Ruby and Emily in the school hall, listening to the Year 9s singing madrigals, Jo pondered on how different she felt to yesterday. Then she hadn't wanted to chat to Ruby about anything at all and had felt as if she hated Emily for stealing Stuart. Now, Emily was back to being second-best-buddy and the three girls couldn't stop chattering (albeit in whispers) about their promised holiday together in Brighton.

'I looked A-M-I up on the internet and they are big, I mean BIG…really, this band is going places, and with any luck we'll be one step behind!' said Emily, stars of ambition shining in her eyes.

'Well, I'm not sure about one step behind,' said Ruby, 'but the open mic event will be a great opportunity to play to an audience who don't know us. And

Brighton, there's so many big names that live in Brighton.' The more practical down-to-earth Ruby was almost as excited as Emily.

'I'm so glad Stuart can come too,' said Jo, generously, for some reason, no longer feeling any malice towards him.

'Me too, of course,' said Emily. 'But who was that dishy bloke I saw you swapping phone numbers with in the shop at the Globe yesterday?'

'Emily you were spying on me!'

'No…you weren't exactly in a secret place, millions of tourists milling around. Who was he?'

'Oh he was just a guy I bumped into in the queue going in. I didn't give him my real phone number. I don't even know why he wanted my number.' Jo got rid of any intrigue around Alex as quickly as she could.

'Oh Jo, why didn't you give him your real number?' asked Emily.

'He lives in Edinburgh!'

'No matter,' said Ruby. 'Edinburgh would be great place to visit'.

When Jo got back home from school, she took her costume upstairs and hung it up. She had carried it carefully all the way home in its own bag, instead of squashing it in with her other stuff. Grandma and Ollie were out at Ollie's last choir practice before the summer break. Ollie had a brilliant voice which had not broken yet and he was a valued chorister for Magdalen College choir.

As she switched on her laptop, Jo knew what she was going to see and she wasn't wrong: a message from Mela flashed up, saying 'hello' and that she had tried to get in touch the evening before. Then scrolling down from that came the formal message from SHARP. Almost the same as the one she had received six months before. But not quite. They were clearly making an effort to make her feel important, which was a bit strange after nothing for a whole six months. Still now they were back and excitement fizzled through her from head to toe. She carefully read through to see if she could spot any changes.

‹WELCOME ONCE AGAIN, JO TO THE SCIENTIFIC HISTORY AND ART RECLAMATION PROGRAMME 15800›

‹SHARP Instructions and Policy Information›
You have a full copy of our policy from your previous involvement with us. It has not changed. We still hold

firm in the belief that it is possible to travel back safely through time to bring about the greater good for all humanity past and present.

‹Pre-Travel Information›

You have a different phone now to the one that we contacted you on previously and so we have had to make some adjustments. As before, your mobile phone is specially modified to act as a time travel device. We have fitted it with some necessary apps, activated by the three new icons on your screen: a black phoenix, a green phoenix and a red phoenix. Press the black phoenix for information and to communicate with SHARP. If you wish to accept a time travel mission that we offer you, press the green phoenix and then enter your unique SHARP project number 15800: the system will be activated and you will be transported back in time. When it is time to return you will feel your phone vibrating. Take the phone out of the travel bag, press the red phoenix and enter your project number. If you need to return, because of danger before the phone vibrates, press the red phoenix and enter your project number. This should only be done under real emergency conditions.

‹Travel Information›

We cannot emphasize enough the importance of being alone and somewhere safe before setting out, and of no one missing you. We are still aiming at our young 21st century time travellers only being away from their own time for four to six minutes. This allows for several hours or possibly days in the time they have travelled back to. However, under difficult conditions, the time away in your present might be longer. Because of this, try to **make absolutely sure** no one is likely to notice or be worried by your departure. Sloppiness in this respect can be very bad for all concerned.

Jo back tracked and read all the information again. She knew there had never been a time when she had caused worry to her family, but…

Our scientists have been working wonders with the time/space travel bag and it is now lighter and more flexible than ever. When it is stuck to your side, you really will not feel it. Remember to do this before you leave. We have had trouble with a time traveller forgetting to do this and so they did not have the camera disc with them or anywhere to keep their mobile safe. Remember, on arrival, however dreamy or dozy you feel, (and we do know this is one of the effects of time travel), take the silver disc out and press it to your forehead. When the backing disc comes away leaving just the film, do put the discarded disc back in the bag. These are actually quite expensive and easily reusable.

‹Return Journey›

We appreciate that there can be dangerous situations and the **emergency procedure** of pressing the red phoenix icon and then keying in your dedicated number of **15800** sometimes has to be used, but do try to only come back when you feel the phone vibrating which means that your return has been activated by us in the most cost- effective way.

‹After Your Visit›

We will, of course, contact you after your trip to let you know how you have done. Rest assured that your safety is of the upmost importance to us and without you and other young people trusting us and travelling back in time, the world and civilization as you know it would be lost.

The screen went blank and Jo sat for a minute without moving. What did they mean, she wondered about the future of the world and civilization being lost? Did they say that last time? She certainly couldn't remember it if they had.

Then Mela's voice came in on her mobile.

'Are you OK Jo?'

'I think so, but what did SHARP mean in that last sentence about the world and civilization being lost? I don't remember anything like that last time.'

'What happens is that when we first contact you, we tell you about how all the world's records, books, writing, computer files ,etc were destroyed in something we call the Dark Chaos. All that is true, perfectly true, but what we don't tell you is that it is a little more complicated than that.'

'But you can explain it to me can't you. I can't take on something I don't know about fully'.

'Of course, I understand, Jo. To put it simply, what people in the twenty-first century haven't yet discovered, although they are maybe getting close, is that every kind or unkind deed leaves behind a trace – an un-erasable trace in the dimensions of space in which the world exists. The traces that kind deeds leave are benign, but those from unkind, bad, evil deeds can gather together and make something like a rip in the fabric of the dimension in which the earth exists, and through this rip more bad stuff can come. When you put on the camera film, we at SHARP can see the traces and the rips in the universe and we have the technology to, put very simply again, mend them'.

'Oh my goodness! This is serious stuff'.

'Yes, it is, that is why we don't tell you at the start.'

'But when I went back last time, there were no bad people there.'

'No ,and there won't be this time, but what you have to realise is that when there are very creative people – artists, writers, musicians and so on, whose minds are wholly taken up by their art, there are always people who are jealous of that creativity or those who want to use if for their own ends. We have discovered that many of the instigators of the Nazi war machine had huge artistic interests, for instance. And jealousy itself can be a very potent force for evil.'

Jo didn't answer for a while and then said quietly: 'I felt jealous of Emily and Stuart when they got together.'

There was a short laugh from Mela.

'Yes, but you wouldn't stick a knife in either of

them would you? Or stop them getting on in the world by trickery? Or tell slanderous things about them would you?'

'No, of course not.'

'Exactly, we all have bad feelings, bad thoughts, temptations etcetera – it's all part of being human, but the traces left behind in the time/space dimension are not caused by those, they are caused by bad, evil, unkind, call it what you like, thoughts that lead to actions. Think of Macbeth, all his tortured thinking about murder, his 'is this a dagger I see before me' murderous thoughts would have been just that, if he had not done the deed.'

'I see, so thoughts in themselves aren't bad but acting on them is.'

'Exactly. Now Jo, I've not much time left and you have got to decide if you want to go back in time for SHARP again, but before the details come up about your next travel option, you must listen to me carefully, I mean really carefully.'

'I will, Mela. I'm paying attention.'

'Well, you remember last time when you met the great writers in Oxford, C.S. Lewis and Tolkien, your position, the validity of what you were saying was suspected by Tolkein.'

'Of course I remember.'

'His sensitive, intuitive mind picked up that you were not of their time and we had a lot of difficulty? Transmission was broken. That was caused in part because you were so overwhelmed by meeting these literary giants, and it was partly my fault for not warning you enough. I should have realised that it would be difficult for you not to be bowled over by meeting them.'

'I certainly was, that is true and I am so sorry.'

'No need to be, as I said, it was partly my fault. Your age is very strange about revering special people, you call them celebrities, and give them what seems to us at SHARP almost ridiculous importance. Anyone who's maybe sung in some kind of band or something, played one of your sports better than others or done something that gets them on one of your screens suddenly becomes one of these celebrities – even people who cook food! Or people who go somewhere horrid and eat horrid stuff get to be one of these celebrities.'

By now Jo was laughing a little. 'And do you find that strange?' she asked.

'It would take me ages to explain how strange we find it.' Mela paused… 'But I must continue. If you are sent back to meet someone whose fame has lasted over the years, you must rid your mind of what you know about them as much as possible and try not to intimate in any way to them what the future might hold. You are going back in time for the reasons I have just told you. BUT, and definitely for you this time, also to give encouragement, help, support and kindness to the people that you meet. Those attributes will cross the time gap and you will be able to help that person, but only if they see you as someone perfectly normal. The person you are going to meet on this occasion, although only young, is even more intuitive than Tolkien. Do you understand Jo?'

Jo felt a shiver go through her, it all seemed so very important. 'Who am I meeting on this trip?'

'You will see that in a second on the travel options. Now a couple more things...' Mela was speaking really quickly now. 'Firstly, your equipment will include a small earpiece. It fits into your ear perfectly and works as a translator for both what you hear and what you say. Without it you would not be able to understand the English spoken by the people in the part of the country you are going to and the time period you will be in.

Secondly, unlike your other times, you are going to go back in time fully clothed. Put on the excellent costume your grandma has made; her research was exact, and you will definitely pass as a young girl from the Elizabethan merchant class. So before you click the green icon, Jo, when you are in your costume, **think yourself** into the part. We feel sure that it will help you enormously, think yourself into the part you must play and the time you will be in.'

Mela switched off abruptly without saying good-bye, as if her time had run out.

Jo was shaking with excitement, stood still for a moment and then saw that the screen had lit up. She started to read:

‹Details of Current Travel Option›

‹Time Zone›

Summer, 1577.

‹Place›

Stratford-upon-Avon in Warwickshire.

‹Landing›

The edge of a small wood near the town close to the River Avon.

‹Instructions›

On landing, look for a basket containing two small plants; one is the speedwell, believed to cure back ache and other ailments if drunk in an infusion, the other is common wild thyme. Take this basket with you.

‹Destination›

Follow the small path through the wood until you meet a thirteen- year- old boy. His name is William Shake-speare.

At this point Jo stopped reading and let out a gasp and shook her head, as if not believing what she was reading.

‹Conditions›

Favourable. Weather warm. No war or risk of disease.

‹Identity›

A young girl from the merchant class, coming from a village nearby called Shotterly. Your family are friends with the family of Anne Hathaway who the thirteen-year-old Shakespeare has already met (because this family are known to his mother). Your older brother is friends with Anne's brother Bartholomew. You have been sent by your mother to gather some wild flowers,

in particular, the two specimens that are in the basket
(See above).

‹Equipment›

Mobile phone, time/space travel bag and translator
earpiece.

If you wish to travel, do as follows:

› First make sure you have memorised the above
  details for travel very carefully. Then change into
  the Elizabethan costume made by your grand
  mother. Most unusually, wear this costume to
  travel. Then put in the earpiece.

› Press the time/space travel bag close to your
  body so that it is attached.

› Press the green phoenix icon on your mobile.

› Tap in the project number **15800**.

Good luck with this vital mission.

Then the screen went blank.

For quite some minutes, Jo couldn't move because she was trembling so much, but then she managed to calm herself down. She attached the
time/space travel bag to her skin below her ribs, where

it stuck firmly but painlessly in place. Then she slipped her costume over her head. The struggle to tie up the laces of the tight-fitting bodice really helped to get rid of the jitters. She remembered asking her grandma to put the laces at the front so they would easier to do up. 'Oh no,' Grandma had said, 'that would never do, front lacing was for the yeomanry and the poor; lacing at the back meant that you had servants to help you.' Grandma had gone on to explain that everything about the clothes that Elizabethans wore told others something of their situation and place in the world. The colour of Jo's dress was a rich, deep, apricot. Jo would have preferred blue, but that wouldn't do for the same reason as the front lacing; blue was a cheap dye and so was worn more often by servants or the poor.

When she had finished getting the costume right and tying the band of ribbon, that was in the same colour as her dress, round her head, Jo looked at herself in the mirror. As her reflection stared back at her, she straightened her back and felt something in her mind shift. The longer she stared at her reflection, the more she felt her twenty-first century persona slipping away. She picked up her mobile, pressed the green phoenix icon and then dialled 15800. The sound, that she remembered so well, started off far away and then, as it came nearer, became an ear-splitting, high-pitched whine. Then... Nothing.

CHAPTER 5

A Bank Whereon The Wild Thyme Grows

The ground shifted slightly beneath her and Jo looked down. The carpet beneath her feet was not the one in her bedroom but one of soft, green moss. In front of her was no bedroom mirror but a thickly wooded area and, behind her, a field where sheep were grazing, and then beyond that a small half-timbered farmhouse. She could just see that in the garden to one side of the house, a woman was bent double pulling up weeds from what must be a vegetable patch. Jo remained still for some time, recovering from the shock of travelling through time and space. Just as SHARP warned, she was suffering from time slip; her head swimming with thoughts that were jumping in and out of her mind in a hopeless jumble.

'I must concentrate, concentrate,' she murmured over and over again.

The beauty of the wood, which was made up of huge, ancient-looking oak trees, slowly began to infiltrate her swirling mind. High overhead, a midday sun was blazing down, but just where she stood, a cool breeze rustled through the leaves. Such quiet, such peace – even the birds were scarcely to be heard in this suspended space. Jo stood, stared and then almost as if hypnotised, moved towards the nearest tree, placed her hand on it and, without knowing why, pressed her face against the rough bark and circled her arms round the trunk, which was far too wide for her hands to meet. This made her remember that, in one hand, she was holding her mobile.

She walked forward into the trees a little, so that should the busy gardener look up, she would not be seen. Sitting down in a corner where the massive roots of the tree branched and sunk down into the earth, Jo fished under her costume to find the time/space travel bag. She slipped the camera disc out and pressed it to her forehead, just above the ribbon that circled her brow. The thin film stuck to her skin while the backing came away easily. With slightly trembling fingers, she put the disc in the bag and her mobile with it. Now that the time slip was easing, a new emotion was taking her over – if SHARP were correct, when she walked through this wood she would come face to face with the boy who would one day become a playwright that almost everyone, including her parents and teachers, thought of as the greatest playwright that had ever lived. It made her feel sick with apprehension. She clung on to what Mela had said about meeting famous people from the past:

'You must rid your mind of what you know about them as much as possible. You must think yourself into the time you are in. A girl in 1577 would not have been overawed by a thirteen-year-old boy, especially as you, at fourteen, are one year older.'

Breathing deeply to calm herself, she stood up and looked through the trees to try and make out a pathway but couldn't see one. Opposite her, propped up against a tree trunk, was a small roughly woven basket. Retrieving it as her own property, she looked inside.

'Now which of you two rather miserable specimens is Speedwell and which of you is Wild Thyme? Is it you with this small limp stem and tiny blue flowers? Or is it you with these slightly bigger, more jolly, darker mauve flowers? It would have been handy to have you labeled.' Jo was enjoying her conversation with her herbs. 'Never mind being a girl from Elizabethan times, I think I've turned into Alice in Wonderland. After all, falling down a rabbit hole and landing in what can only be described as an alternative universe is not so different to this time travelling thingy, is it?' Jo's conversation with herself was doing her good. Her nerves had vanished and she was in the mood to enjoy whatever should happen next.

She wandered deeper into the wood, still chattering to herself about rabbits and Cheshire cats. Then she saw the path, it came from a little to the right of where she had landed. There was nothing much to mark it except that a few trees had been lopped down to indicate its route and the ground was slightly beaten down by feet that had gone before. She followed the path for a good ten minutes and was beginning to wonder if she had remembered the instructions correctly, when she felt something land on her head. It fell at her feet and she bent down to pick up a small bundle of twigs bound together with some grass stems. She stood up straight away, turned round and looked up, expecting to see someone in the branches of the tree behind her. There was no one. Puzzled she carried on walking a few steps and then heard a voice calling out: 'Not everything is as it seems.'

She swiveled round and looked at the upper branches of the tree behind her, where she suspected someone was hiding.

'Don't let your eyes deceive you,' came the voice

again, wafting down from up high.

'I'm not. I can see your hand gripping one side of the trunk of that tree perfectly well,' she called back, grinning to herself because she could see no such thing.

There followed a lot of scrabbling noises, some leaves showering down, together with a few exclamations and words that were probably curses that weren't in her special earpiece database, and then a loud thump as a boy landed on his feet but then collapsed in heap on the ground. When he got up and came towards her, Jo saw that he was not much taller than her brother Ollie and had the most wonderful, mischievous eyes she had ever seen.

Near to her, he stopped and looked puzzled. His smile switched off, and he gave her a brief clumsy bow.

'I'm sorry, young maid, I owe you an apology. I thought I knew you because you looked so like someone else I know, from above that is…I'd been looking for her… but I can see now that you are younger than she. I have never met you before so do not know your name.'

Jo, wanting to put him at his ease as he looked so crestfallen, said without thinking, 'Well, I know your name: you're the *famous* William Shakespeare!'

Far from reassuring her, the boy stepped back. He looked shocked and when he did speak his voice was no longer jolly but tense, and unfriendly:

'You mean **infamous** I assume, maid, not famous! Please choose your words either more carefully, or at least more tactfully. Words like infamous and worse are being bandied all around Stratford-upon-Avon already, bringing constant pain, sadness, bitterness and unjust shame upon my family – simply because my father no longer has the income in these harsh times. He was always and still is the best of men.'

Now Jo had to try and apologise and it was hard to do because she realised that, in one brief moment of meeting William Shakespeare, she had completely forgotten everything she had been told. She had fallen into such a stupid trap. Why on earth had she let slip she knew his name? Now she had to try to convince him that she had meant no harm with very little information to back up what she needed to say; she had read on the internet that Shakespeare's father had, at one time, been very important in the town, wealthy and on something like their town council, but then he had lost his fortune, that must be what the boy Will was upset about.

Her words tumbled out a chaotic babble: 'Of course I did not mean 'infamous'! To me, you and your family are famous.' (Oh, she thought, perhaps I shouldn't have said that) but she carried on. 'I know how misjudged your family has been of late, of course I do. But believe me, none of your real friends think ill of you or your family and the best of them constantly remind those tittle-tattling gossips just how much they all owe to your father.' Jo paused again, this time because she couldn't tell from the boy's expression if she had made things any better. 'Your father gave so generously of his time, and money. All revere your father... yes revere. I can assure you also that the poor remember and value your family's practical help and many kindnesses. And there is one of my friends who loves you most of all.' Jo's babbling stuttered to a stop. Where had that last sentence come from? She wanted the ground to swallow her up, or at least her mobile to take her back to the twenty-first Century. This meeting with famous people thing was obviously much harder than she had first imagined. It was all SHARP's fault for sending her. They should have chosen someone else, someone brainier.

'Oh, oh, methinks you do protest too much.' A

smile had spread across his face and his voice took on a teasing tone: 'Yes, much too much…I believe you; there are some that do not slander us and anyway, the day is much too fine a day to waste it hating, what did you call them?… 'tittle-tattling gossips'… oh I must remember those words.' A big grin spread across his face. 'Yes tittle-tattling gossips, I will use it myself.'

'Really?' asked Jo, immediately brightening up.

'And now we are on to names, you can call me Will, everyone does.' The boy gave her a small bow and Jo, to her complete amazement, found herself blushing and bobbing in a small curtsey of all things! At home she would die rather than curtsey to boy!

He smiled again, and then continued, 'And I am going to guess your name.'

'You are?' asked Jo, suddenly aware that SHARP, as usual, had failed to give her the name she should have.

'Yes, I think your name is Susanna, and you and your family live a short way off from my mother's friends, at Shottery, or thereabouts.'

'You are right,' said Jo remembering the name Shottery from SHARP's instructions, even if they had forgotten to give her something as important as her name.

'And I can tell you,' Will went on with enthusiasm bubbling in his voice, 'that Susanna is one of my favourite names – not, you understand my most favourite name, that begins with…an A , it does indeed. Now tell me, where are you going to with your basket?' He leant over and peered into the basket and nodded, as if not at all surprised to see what she had in there.

'Ahh, I see you are planning on culling simples.'

Jo gave her left ear a slight rub. The translator in her ear didn't seem to be doing a very good job. What were simples? She looked down at the two specimens in her basket; they must be simples – they looked a bit on the simple side.

'My mother has sent me here because she says there is a meadow nearby where these flowers grow.'

'Your mother is right. If you follow the path through the trees, you will come to the water meadows of the Avon, but do you know where to look for them?'

'I'm afraid I do not.'

'Well, then your search will take you a good long time, especially for this fellow.' Will held up one of the plants. 'Oh what a poorly, wilting one this is!' He held the specimen out for them both to inspect. 'The wild thyme does not like too much wet on its roots in winter (when the water might come over the banks and flood the meadow), so it does not grow in the middle of the meadow but higher up on the bank at the edge of the wood. I could show you if you like?'

'That would be most kind of you, Will.'

'Come on then.' He set off along the path at a good speed, Jo's basket dangling from one hand, and Jo scampering alongside him trying to keep up.

When they reached the edge of the wood, they came to a glorious meadow that seemed to be almost like a wild garden to Jo, as so many flowers were scattered in amongst the grass. They gathered the speedwell flowers first, searching the tall grass that hid the smaller plant with its pale blue flowers. Then, Will led them back towards a part of the wood where the ground was a bit higher, forming a gentle, sloping bank. It was shaded by the branches of trees stretching out towards the meadow. Here, Will pointed to the pretty clusters of Thyme. Because they grew closely together, it was easy for Jo to pick them quickly, but Will had stopped helping. He had sat down on the bank and was staring absently out across the meadow, occasionally looking upwards to the sky at the small fluttering dot of a skylark, which was filling their ears with its splendid trilling.

'You would not have found these without me, would you?'

Jo looked up quickly. His voice had changed; there was a hard edged tone to it.

'No, I most certainly would not have done, and I am very grateful to you,' Jo stopped picking the flowers and went to sit down beside him, but not too close.

'So what a good job I walked out of school today – walked out and left them to it I did.' Will's expression had changed to a dark angry frown.

'You walked out of school in the middle of the day! Surely you will be in a lot of trouble for doing that?'

'This morning I could take it no more. We have a meal break for two hours at eleven o'clock. We had only just taken our places at the table when the sniggering began, whispered insults, name calling, being jostled. And when I finished my meal someone stuck out a leg to trip me up as I left the room. It's the same every day.'

'You are being bullied!' said Jo, aghast.

'It's been going on for a while now.'

'Have you told the teachers, I mean the master at the school?'

'They are no use. They take no notice of such things. I get so angry, Susanna, I could punch one of the dog-hearted, clay-brained toads. ' (Despite herself, Jo had to smother a smile at the names he made up that insulted others so well.)

'I haven't done anything so far, because I know they are waiting to see me get so angry I start a fight, and then they would all be on to me.'

'You have been clever, Will; that is the way to deal with bullies.'

'What do you know of it? Girls do not have to face going to school.'

'Noo… but my father has told me that when he was at school, he was bullied and that he ignored the bullies, taking as little notice of them as possible, and after a while they got fed up.' Jo longed to say more; to give Will all the twenty-first century thinking on bullying, which despite its good psychology and good intentions, still hadn't got rid of it.

'But as for girls not having to face school, I would dearly love to have to go to school.'

'Would you?'

'Yes, of course, isn't there so much to learn, so many wonderful things to find out about?'

'You are right, of course, but today I have resolved never to go back there!' Will flung out an arm as if making a proclamation.

'You can't mean that! That would be terrible. You wouldn't… you wouldn't…' what Jo wanted to say was wouldn't have enough knowledge to write all your wonderful plays but instead she finished with 'fulfill your true potential.'

'Would I not? I do not know if I have any potential.'

Jo felt as if she might explode as the names of all Shakespeare's plays flooded her brain.

'Err, err… what about your poems, you have written good poems have you not?'

'Oh, that is what really did it for me today. The schoolmaster that I admire the most, for he is a good poet, returned one of my poems to me at the start of school and said, and these were his words exactly:

'Master William Shakespeare, I think you would be better employed feeding seed to the chickens of your household than putting pen to paper.''

'He said that!' exclaimed Jo.

'That was a worse insult to me than anything those boys could say.'

For a moment Jo did not know what to say. And then it came to her, remembering how her mother had told her that she had had lot of trouble at university because one of her tutors seemed to have a down on her and in the end she thought it was jealousy, fearing her student would go farther in her work than she had. She turned to Will and took hold of his arm.

'This is important, Will. I am older than you and sometimes, you know, girls can see things that boys miss,' she paused and he turned to look at her. She returned his gaze steadily.

'This master at your school, you said he is a good poet?'

'Yes, he is quite a good poet.'

'Exactly Will, **quite a good** poet – and in a hundred years no one will have heard of him. You are not quite a good poet, you are an extraordinarily good poet.' Jo stopped fearing that if she added any more she would jeopardise the camera connection to SHARP, as had happened with Tolkien. But she had said enough. Will had cheered immensely.

'Jealous of me, jealous of me, I think you may be right! What a very perceptive girl you are! I will return to school tomorrow. I will continue my lessons. But how will I explain that I left so abruptly today?'

'Oh that's easy,' said Jo, clutching her forehead and clutching her stomach. 'I had such a pain in my head and I had such a pain in my stomach, I thought I would be sick all over everyone! So I left quickly to save you all! That would not be hard for you to do would it? I think, maybe, you might be a good actor as well as a good poet?'

'I am, yes, certainly I am. Not only perceptive, you are a splendid muse for good ideas. Here, take this and when you are alone you can read the poem. I had intended to give this to that very same Master this morning. Now you can read it and... maybe share it with any of your good friends in Shotterly.'

Jo looked down at a folded piece of parchment paper sealed with a blob of wax. Her mind went into shock as she realised that William Shakespeare was handing her a poem. She could not refuse to take it; he would take that as another snub to his talents. She reached out her hand and tucked the poem into the pocket of her dress.

They didn't say anything more for a while, but walked quietly towards the river and, Jo guessed, towards the town. Then suddenly, they both became aware of a distant raucous noise, the beating of a drum, loud calls and music coming from the direction of the houses and church spire that were just coming into view between the trees.

'Listen, my new friend Susanna.' Will stopped and turned to face her, his face lighting up with excitement, 'What can you hear in the distance?

CHAPTER 6

Singers, Clowns, Long Speeches And Sword Fights

Jo shook her head, not knowing what the sounds they heard could mean.

'It's the travelling players!' Will exclaimed.

'The travelling players?' Jo repeated.

Will took no notice of her question but carried on: 'Now I remember Susanna – this is their day to perform in the courtyard of the tavern. The renowned troupe of players that is known as Leicester's Men are come to Stratford! It's been up on large banners for the past four days. I've been so consumed by my stupid worries that I have walked by, scarcely noticing. Come on, if we run, we may be able to watch from side stage. It's the best place to be.'

He caught her hand and whirled her around and around, laughing exuberantly. 'I bet you have never seen a performance before have you?' Still holding hands, they ran down through the middle of the field, under the shady archway and onto the embankment of the river Avon, the hubbub of high-spirited sound coming nearer and nearer as they raced along a tree-cooled pathway. Jo struggled to keep up, hot in the cumbersome dress, her legs unaccustomed to the entanglements of long skirt.

They slowed when they neared the market place. At first, it seemed to Jo like a picture postcard come to life but, as she looked around, she realised it was not picture postcard prettiness – she was looking at a working Elizabethan town. Yes, the houses had huge, wooden beams criss-crossed among the plaster but they were not painted white; they were a dirty, muddy brown. The top stories jutted out over the roadway, just as Jo had seen in Elizabethan properties with preservation orders on them, and people were sitting on window sills looking down at the scene below. That looks charming, she thought, until a splash of something or other she didn't want to think about splattered on the roadway in front of her. It had come from a bowl emptied from above without any thought that someone might be below. Disgusting!

A group of musicians in brightly coloured costumes were playing. What were those instruments? Jo didn't recognize any of them, other than the two that looked quite like violins and, of course, the drum. She listened and was captivated; the catchy tune and bouncy beat made her feet want to dance.

Already the citizens of Stratford- upon-Avon were gathering in clusters in their favourite spots, greeting friends and seemingly, Jo thought, catching up with local news. Unceremoniously, Will pushed his way through the crowd, still hanging on to Jo's hand. As she passed a thick-set man, he punctuated his talk to another with a huge, emphatic gob of spit that just missed Jo's cheek, landing on dusty ground! And oh, the whiff, the pong coming from the bodies around! Her nostrils were assaulted by smells she had never smelt before, and never wanted to smell again! Will headed towards the front of the rough staging the players had constructed, no doubt in the early morning. The stage jutted out from the inn and Will stopped on the far side, where the space at the side of the stage extension was less crowded. As they took their place next to a man and woman dressed quite finely, Jo found her eyes drawn to the woman's face. No, she mustn't stare! The woman, who was really pretty with dark brown curls tumbling over her shoulders, had pitted marks on her skin, some a dull, angry red. Jo shuddered, she knew what those pock marks on the woman's face meant: the woman had recovered from smallpox and perhaps not that long ago because she suddenly said quite audibly to the man she was with, 'Dearest husband, I cannot stay, I still feel too weak. You stay and enjoy some revelry. Return home later to me.' Their eyes followed her, as the woman left her husband's side, and a wave of sympathy smothered Jo's high spirits for a moment.

The music of the players was now so close and loud that it was no surprise that the pre-performance entertainment was about to begin. Soon dancers, musicians, actors and clowns, all wearing bright, gaudy outfits cavorted their way through the assembled crowds. With each new appearance shouts, cheers and a welcome waving-of-kerchiefs surged up from the crowd. Jo glanced at Will. He was entranced by the spectacle, his face glowing with joy as he watched the changing performers. He was in another world.

When each group had paraded to a noisy welcome, they all clambered on to the temporary stage, filling up the edges and freezing into a suitable pose of their own choice. They held the pose like statues, not moving so much as an eyelid to blink. When all the players were grouped on the stage, a man, dressed in especially fine and colourful clothes, entered from back stage to centre stage. He swept off his hat with a flourish and bowed low to the, now hushed, audience.

Replacing his hat with great care and elegance, he also struck a pose and introduced, in turn, the dancers, the singers, the clowns and then the actors: it was all a joyful romp and the crowd clapped, laughed and roared their approval. Then most of the performers left the stage, for the play proper was about to begin. Before he left, the handsome 'warm-up' man turned towards Will and gave him a quick wink.

'Do you know that man, Will? I'm sure he winked at you like a friend, only not quite...'

'Indeed I do. He is James Burbage, no less: one of the greatest of the travelling actors. He has been chosen by Lord Dudley to lead this troupe. They are known as Leicester's Men. Sometimes in the past, when the players are in or near Stratford, I help out. I mean I'll help any of the actors who wish me to work for them before, during or after the performance, on stage or off. There is usually at least one or two people looking for likely all-purpose boys who can be trusted to take tickets, show newcomers where there is still space, stand in as crowd actors, be girls instead of boys, for no girl has ever been allowed on this stage, and so on... Where have you been these last thirteen years, Susanna, that you know not these things?'

'At home, Will, not here in Stratford,' Jo replied,

smiling to herself that at least she was being truthful there.

'Yes, sorry, I do forget how different it is for girls sometimes. And not everyone likes these entertainments as much as I do. No one in my family bothers to come to see them and they don't understand why I love plays so much. I usually come as often as I can and sometimes the players offer me a small part. I am brilliant at playing the part of a girl, even if you do think I don't understand them that well.'

'I'm sure you are a very good girl,' said Jo, giggling, which resulted in Will giving her an indignant dig in the ribs with an elbow.

'Anyway, now I am full thirteen they entrust me with many other jobs, both on or off the stage, as I care not what I do. In the history sketches for instance, I make a good squire to their knight. But we must be quiet now for the prologue is about to start.'

The tall man dressed in the fine clothes came back on the stage. He now had a very commanding presence, and his voice rang out loud and clear above the heads of the crowd. Jo found the prologue hard to follow but gathered that its main purpose was to give the audience the understanding that what they were about to see would be a tragic story in which most of the participants would lose their lives but that the hero would die knowing that '…a maid more fair than the blossom in spring or that any poet could describe…' had loved him and supposedly would remain faithful to his memory forever.

Jo whispered, 'it sounds as if there is going to be a lot of killing.'

'Yes, but shush, the deep stuff begins...' Jo shushed. The deep stuff began. There were lots of lengthy speeches, which Jo couldn't follow, and lots of grim, wildly frantic sword fights scattered like lightening slashes through the play...well half a play, for suddenly, at a frenzied moment in the unfolding tragedy, it petered out and the actors suddenly broke into a comic song and dance routine, then lined up for applause. The audience roared their approval. When the din died down, Jo burst out perplexed:

'That didn't seem like a proper ending. Surely they have stopped too soon?'

'Yes, you are right, the play is only half way through. Most play writers often, or usually, send out the first half of their script before they have written the second. It is of benefit to them. The players have longer to learn their lines, the breaking point will end the first half at an exciting moment in the plot and the audience applause – or lack of it – is a guide to the playwright as to whether the second half is on course to bring a goodly audience back, on their next visit to the town.'

'Oh, I see,' said Jo. Then noticing that most of the crowd at the front of the stage was beginning to disperse added sadly, 'Perhaps we should make our way home now.' Will took no notice of this comment but carried on explaining the players' and playwrights' ways.

'It also benefits the writer as well, you see, as he has another month or two or three to finish the play. Well, this is only the first performance of the day. If the second is as well received, they might even decide on three performances tomorrow.'

'When you will be at school,' said Jo in as stern a voice as she could muster.

'Certainly, I'll be at school tomorrow,' replied Will, clutching his stomach and bending over, as if to be sick in order to convince Jo he knew what he had to do to get back into school without any trouble. While he was still doubled up, the head of a small boy appeared around the side of the stage.

'Will, are you not well, my friend?' asked the boy, jumping down off the stage and looking at Will with concern.

Will straightened himself up and laughed. 'The excellent Master Burbage, nine or ten years old or thereabouts. Master Richard Burbage, this is my friend Susanna.'

Jo found herself holding the hand of a small, round-faced boy who gave her a deep bow while she bobbed the required curtsey! Life could not get stranger.

'So, Will, if you are not sick then, will you be coming to help out my father's troop tomorrow?' asked Richard Burbage.

There was a sigh from Will as he shook his head. 'No Richard, it is Latin and more Latin and more Latin for me tomorrow. And now I must be getting this young maid back on the path she must take to her home. She has a bit of a way to walk and we don't want the night goblins to come out and get her do we?'

Both Shakespeare and the boy started pulling scary faces at each other and whispered the words, 'night goblins' in goblin voices. They circled around Jo and pulled ever more grotesque faces. Jo, guessing this was something they had done before, pleased them by acting scared. Then they straightened up and laughed together. Will flung a quick, friendly arm around the smaller boy's shoulders and then lifted him back up onto the stage. 'Go and tell your father, I am at school tomorrow, sadly.'

They waited at the side of the stage a little longer to make sure that most of the townspeople had gone on their way home, so that no one should spot that Will was not in school and take the news back to his mother and father. When they were sure it was safe, they set off in the direction they had come.

'You no longer have your basket with you.' Will remarked.

'No, I set it down by the bank where the wild thyme grew, thinking I'd pick it up on my way back.'

'That was a good idea, but we must retrace our steps now as quickly as we can.'

They walked back in a friendly, but serious, silence. It was as if, somehow, the adult world had suddenly intruded on a strange, magical childhood adventure. Evening shadows were beginning to lengthen a little. When they got back to the basket, Jo picked it up and tried to reassure Will that she would be fine walking back through wood on her own, but he was having none of it.

'It's still daylight, and I will be fine,' Jo insisted.

'I am coming with you until you are safely on the

road to Shottery.' Will stated firmly.

Twenty minutes later, Jo found out that the 'road to Shottery' was a small, dusty track that ran past the farm where she had seen the woman in the garden weeding, what now seemed like years before.'

'Time is a very strange thing,' she said to the young boy beside her.

'Yes, it is very strange, I swear it plays tricks on us. In a minute or two, I am going to take your hand to say goodbye, but I feel as if I have known you all my life, and,' he sighed, 'for some reason that I cannot explain, I feel that I may never see you again.'

Jo shivered and dipped her hand into her pocket. Now was the time she should take out the poem and give it back to its owner, and she was just about to do it when his next words stopped her.

'Please keep the poem I gave you. If it is in your safekeeping, I know I will remember what you have said and I will stay strong and not let the jealousy of others destroy me, or deflect me from my path.' With that, Will bowed to her, leant forward and softly,kissed her cheek; then he set off across the field towards the woods without looking back.

Jo stood still for quite some time watching the thirteen-year-old William Shakespeare walk back up to the wood and eventually disappear into the trees. In her mind, he was no longer the boy who would become a famous playwright, now he was someone with whom she had shared – what? How would she ever be able to explain what she had shared and why she was now beginning to feel a loss, a small, niggling pain growing somewhere inside her. She realised she still held the basket with its cargo of plants. She set it down at a little gate in the small fence that ran around the farm. Perhaps the 'simples' would be of use to the hard-working farmer's wife. Unsure of what to do next and for want of a better idea, she wandered along the dusty track in the direction of the village where she was supposed to live. How nice it would be, she thought, if down the road there was a house where a door would open for her and a family waited to welcome her in. It was time for her to go back to the twenty-first century, and just as a slight surge of panic was beginning to infiltrate her mind, her phone started to vibrate. Quickly fishing under the skirts and undergarments, Jo pulled her phone out of the bag. She looked at this now seemingly strange artefact – had she begun to become an Elizabethan already? She pressed the red phoenix and keyed in her number. She heard the high-pitched whine coming nearer and nearer until her mind blanked out. Then... Nothing.

CHAPTER 7

Smallpox

After she had taken off her costume and hung it back up in the wardrobe, Jo got into bed and pulled the covers over her head. She heard her grandma and Ollie come in the house. Ollie went into the lounge and switched on the TV. Grandma went into the kitchen and, from the sounds coming from that direction, was beginning to prepare tea. Jo stayed under her bedcovers, the niggling pain she had felt before she left 1577 had grown and she was feeling hot and feverish.

'Jo are you up there? Did you have a good day?' Grandma stood at the bottom of the stairs and called up.

'Fine, Grandma,' Jo called back in as loud a voice as she could manage. But she wasn't fine – She was feeling less and less fine by the minute.

'Tea ready in about half an hour.'

'OK, Grandma.' Jo's reply was weaker this time but fortunately seemed to satisfy her grandma who went back into the kitchen.

Jo lay as still as she could. Maybe the pain in her stomach would go away if she didn't move. Suddenly, a piercing, bright pink light filled the room. It concentrated into a dark pink glow and hovered over Jo's bed for several minutes, and then vanished, completely. Her phone went, and from its unique ring tone, she knew it was SHARP.

Jo read the text message from Mela.

We've just checked you out because we were worried our germ barrier had not been working properly for you.

You mean I could have caught some sixteenth century bug? Jo messaged back. Fear flooded through her mind as she remembered the woman with the pock-marked face. Had she caught some dreadful disease that no one would know how to cure? Maybe she was going to get smallpox! Or something even worse!

We always give time travellers a germ barrier shield and on this occasion, unfortunately, it malfunctioned when you were in the market place. The malfunction was for a very short time, but it appears that you did contract something but don't worry. The pink light you have just observed has eliminated all germs, bacteria or viruses that may cause any possible dangers to your health. How are you feeling now?

I still feel awful.

It will take a few hours for your body to adjust to your usual good health. But, I think your fever has gone has it not?

Jo struggled to sit up and look around her. I think it has. I do feel a bit better.

Additionally, we think that you are feeling bad because you are so sensitive to others and your feelings for others on this occasion have been intense. We were aware you might struggle a little with this mission, Jo, which is why we took the unusual step of getting you in contact with another time traveller. You should phone Alex McLean and talk to him. I'll contact you again tomorrow. Goodbye.

The lack of noise, or activity, from Jo's room puzzled her grandma who wondered why the usually

bouncy, lively girl hadn't come bounding down the stairs to tell her about the Elizabethan pageant at her school. After a while, slightly worried, she went up the stairs to investigate. She was even more puzzled to see Jo lying in bed.

'Are you not well, darling?'

Jo sat up and just shook her head miserably. How could she tell her grandma that she had had smallpox but that some advanced medical aid had already zapped it?

Grandma retreated downstairs for the time being but, when she came up half an hour later with her tea, Jo was asleep and she hadn't the heart to wake her up. She didn't disturb her until later in the evening when she took her up a drink of hot chocolate.

'Jo, wake up and let me have a look at you,'

Jo struggled awake and Grandma felt her head, asked her to put out her tongue, professionally checked her pulse (she had done lots of first aid courses in her time) and generally did all those things that people do to try to find out what is wrong with a person who seems ill, finishing up with the time-honoured question, 'Have you got a pain in your tummy?'

Jo shook her head; the pain had now shifted from her stomach to where she thought her heart was.

'I think I have heartache, Grandma,' Jo said in a small voice.

'Oh Jo,' Grandma put her arms around her and gave her warm hug, 'you must be missing your mum and dad.' At which they both started giggling a little – the idea was so absurd.

'I wish it was that,' said Jo. 'But…no…it's not that. I will be glad to see them home, of course,' she added quickly, not wanting to seem disloyal, 'but it isn't that, grandma.'

By now Grandma had quite made up her mind that Jo had fallen for some boy who wasn't returning her feelings, but being 'the-best-grandma-in-the-world' she didn't ask, and just hoped it wasn't the boy in the band called Stuart. She was pretty sure that Stuart and Emily were an item, as they called it.

'How about having a drink of this hot chocolate, Jo, It will make you feel better.'

Jo sat up and took the offered mug. She started to take small sips; her grandma was right, it did make her feel better. Grandma chatted on about her day until Jo had finished the drink.

'What's the time?' Jo asked.

'It's almost ten o'clock, darling. Are you sure you don't want a sandwich? You've had no tea,' Grandma stated this obvious fact as if it was news.

'I don't want anything, honestly.' Jo passed the empty mug back to her grandma and started to slide back down the covers when a guilty thought stopped her and she sat back up again.

'Oh Grandma, I'm so sorry. I haven't told you how everyone said my costume was fantastic.'

'I'm so glad to hear that.'

'You know, Miss Marshal said that if I went back in time, it would be good enough to convince an Elizabethan that I was one of them!' Those hadn't quite been Miss Marshal's words , but Jo couldn't resist trying to let her grandma know just how convincing her work had been.

'That is praise indeed. Now get some sleep, darling, and you'll feel so different in the morning.'

She switched off Jo's light and Jo heard her go into the bathroom.

Hmm, thought Jo, picking up her BlackBerry, ten o'clock is not that late for lads who are on a school trip. The Edinburgh boys are probably still rattling about in their hostel and making their teachers' lives a misery. Should she send a text or phone? Oh no not phone, there was no way she could start a conversation out of the blue with some strange guy the way she was feeling, however much Mela thought that that would help. She sent a quick text message.

Hope you are enjoying the rest of your London trip. Jo

YHA HOSTEL, EUSTON ROAD, LONDON

Sitting around one of the dining tables in the basement kitchen, along with many of the cosmopolitan visitors at their London Youth Hostel, the boys from the Edinburgh secondary school, were feeling very pleased with themselves. They had noticed that their Scots accents seemed to attract a lot of attention, making them more popular than their English counterparts. They were no longer spotty Year 8 boys from Castlemoor Community, but 'young-guys-about-town' with street cred and a mean dress sense. The gaggle of school girls from Spain on the table behind them was definitely interested. Grins, 'where-are-you-from?' questions and ridiculous antics from the boys had all resulted in exaggerated giggles and flashing smiles from the Spanish girls. That was until Mrs Macfarlin, the head of Year 8, came in and shot a look in their direction, which immediately turned them back into spotty boys from Castlemoor Community.

'I thought you all knew that we had asked you to be back in your rooms by ten o'clock.' Mrs MacFarlin's teacher's voice cut through the buzz of conversations in German, Cantonese, French, Spanish, or whatever, with the sharpness of a Scottish dirk.

'Not quite ten o'clock yet, Mrs MacFarlin,' called out Terence, 'ten more minutes to go.'

Mrs MacFarlin consulted her phone reluctantly. 'Correct Terence, but…'

'Aw…give us a bit of leeway here, Mrs MacFarlin,' another boy pleaded.

'We…ll,' amazingly their head of year was wavering.

'We're just discussing what a brilliant day we've had,' put in one bright spark, obviously skilled in diplomatic negotiations with adults.

'Ah yes, that just reminds me, I need an evaluation,' the teacher scanned the assembled crew and her eyes rested on Alex.

'Alex McLean, I might get a few sensible answers out of you. Also, I've been looking for you anyway. Follow me please.'

Alex sighed, disentangled his legs from the cramped space between the table and bench where he was sitting and followed the teacher.

'Teacher's pet,' whispered one of boys, adding to the injustice.

Alex ignored the stupidity and followed Mrs MacFarlin up the stairs to the lounge where most people were quietly accessing the internet on a bank of computers set up against one wall.

'Just before I get to the evaluation questions Alex, could you please send a text to your friend, Alistair, who I am almost sure has left the building. Despite our strict instructions not to do so, he has gone out with Lorraine Peachy, and don't bother trying to cover up for your friend because the girls in Lorraine's dormitory have already given me this information and I have no reason to disbelieve them. I will be speaking strongly to both Lorraine's and Alistair's parents on our return.'

Alex gave another sigh and slipped his iPhone out of his pocket.

'Just tell him that I have requested you to inform him that he must come back to the youth hostel immediately.'

Alex quickly typed in: 'Come back asap, you've been rumbled.' And clicked 'send'.

'Thank you Alex, and now let's get a little evaluation done. First off, which of the historic sites we have visited during our three days in London have you enjoyed the most?'

'The Globe, Mrs MacFarlin, definitely our visit to the Globe.'

Mrs MacFarlin then rattled on for quite some time about how she agreed with his choice and gave lots of reasons for it, all of which she recorded as Alex's responses, much to his relief as it saved him from the necessity of lying; obviously the real reason he had enjoyed it so much was because he had made contact with Jo Kelly.

'Now how about the Tower of London, Alex? What did you think of our visit there?'

'Awesome, Mrs MacFarlin, I mean dungeons and all that. You could feel history oozing out of the place.' A text came in on his phone. He glanced down expecting, Alistair to have sent a reply, but when he saw who it was from, his eyebrows shot up: the text was from Jo Kelly. He excused himself as quickly as he could, telling Mrs MacFarlin that his mother wanted to speak to him.

It was difficult to find an undisturbed spot in a hostel heaving with teenagers, but a downstairs toilet was empty. He quickly dialed Jo's number.

'Thanks for getting in touch so quickly Alex, I

thought it might be difficult for you when you are still on your school trip.'

'It was, believe me. I've a mate who's scooted off into the London night with his girlfriend and a teacher breathing down my neck, not to mention idiot guys who think they are clever.' Alex's good humour and normal, modern day goings-on had a calming effect on Jo.

'I can just imagine,' she said, not quite knowing how to go on next. 'I sent you a text because…because I've no one else to tell.'

'What is it? Have you gone back in time since I saw you at the Globe?'

'Yes, I've only got back here a few hours ago.'

'Phew – wicked. You sound like you're upset though. Did something really bad happen while you were away?'

'No not bad, quite the opposite really.' Then Jo started to tell Alex everything about her time with the young Shakespeare. She got more and more excited as she went on.

Alex realised Jo had made friends with the boy Shakespeare and was now feeling the loss of that friendship. 'I know what you are going through Jo.'

'You do?'

'Yeah, you don't realize it, but you made a friend of the guy that you met, nothing to do really with him becoming a famous playwright later in his life. It's really hard if you make that kind of a friendship. It happened to me when I went back to medieval Scotland. I made a friend called Ian; we did a dangerous climb together and for ages when I got back I just couldn't get him out of my mind. It's something to do with friendship.'

'I think you are right. But there is something else.'

'What?

'Will, the boy I met who was going to grow up into Shakespeare, gave me a poem. I mean I have an original Shakespeare poem in the pocket of my dress.'

There was silence for a minute and then Alex let out whistle. 'My God, Jo what would that be worth!'

'Exactly,'

'Does SHARP know you've got it?'

'No and I don't really want to tell them. You see last time when I went back to Oxford at the time of World War 2, I inadvertently brought something back with me and I got it back to the person it belonged to on my second trip and SHARP never found out. They are very picky about some things.'

'Yes, they can be. But why didn't you give the poem back to him when you were there?'

'I tried to, but he begged me to keep it.'

'So you can.'

'Yes, but I feel really uncomfortable about it. I mean, supposing I kept it for ages and then when I'm grown up, I might be hard up or something and tempted to sell it. I mean it would no doubt be tested, you know carbon dating and stuff and suppose they found out it was genuine…? Supposing I was offered thousands of pounds for it.'

'More like millions, I think, Jo. But don't worry about this just right now. We can think about it in the next few weeks thrash out the moral and ethical rights and wrongs. Look, I've got to go now – Mrs MacFarlin will be on the warpath if I'm not back in the dorm. Has our conversation helped at all? Are you feeling any better?'

'Oh yes, I do feel better, Alex thanks so much. It is so much easier when you can tell someone else about what you are doing isn't it?'

'It is. I told my girlfriend about going back in time.'

'You did?' said Jo, suddenly feeling a little disappointed that Alex had a girlfriend.

'Yes, but now she's living in San Francisco and I doubt I'll ever see her again, but she did seem to understand at the time.'

'SHARP people always say you mustn't tell anyone.'

'I know.'

'But now they seem to think you and I should be talking to each other.'

'Yes, but it's something to do with this special mission.'

'Can I call you again in a few days?'

'I'll text you as soon as I get back home. And don't worry about the poem.'

CHAPTER 8

Olympic Legacy

27TH JULY 2012, EDINBURGH AND OXFORD

At eight minutes past twenty-one hundred hours on the 27th July 2012, while both Jo and Alex were sitting with their families, all eyes glued to the television, they both received a message from SHARP. At the same moment, they both felt their phones throb with the distinctive pulse of a SHARP communication and both stood up and said to the others in the room, 'Got to dash, need the loo,' scooting to the bathroom as quickly as they could. They both read:

A message with instructions for your next mission will be sent to you after the Olympic opening ceremony. No need to reply. By the way, we at SHARP are watching the ceremony from inside the stadium. Impressed.

When Alex got back to the living-room in his family's rather cramped Edinburgh flat, and sat down next to his mum, she put an arm round him and said,

'You've not missed much, Alex. This scene represents the lovely countryside before the smoke and black of the mills and factories came.'

'Aye but there was still a lot of folk who were poor and had a job to scratch a living then,' put in his dad.

'Oh Jock,' his mum countered, 'we all know that, but give this brilliant director some artistic freedom, Remember he set one of his films in Scotland, that doesn't happen very often with British films!'

When Jo returned to the lounge in her family's spacious house in Oxford, her mum raised an eyebrow and mouthed at her, 'Always make-sure you go before a show starts.' Jo had known that her needing the toilet while viewing the television would annoy her mother. And, of course, this particular show was a very special one, as her dad had said, 'A once in a lifetime event.'

She settled down, and despite the excitement of getting a message from SHARP, she was entranced by the countryside scene the producer of the ceremony had recreated. Jo found it wonderful that the wild flowers in the modern setting of a twenty-first-century sports stadium reminded her of the meadows she had seen a week earlier when she had travelled back to 1577. When the carriage with Victorian gentlemen in top hats rolled onto the grassy meadowlands, she couldn't help giving a brief shudder of apprehension, just as the director wanted people to do. The industrial revolution was on its way.

Her parents were still red-eyed and jet-lagged from their flight back from the States. 'We wouldn't miss being in England with our family for the London Olympics, for anything' they had said, smiling at her, Ollie and Grandma, as they had stepped out with their huge suitcases from the airport taxi the previous day.

Now they were knowledgeably giving everyone their interpretation of the scenes unfolding in front of the massive audience at the Olympic stadium. Their joint store of academic knowledge gave them an edge when it came to explaining, or critically assessing, what they were watching. Sometimes, they took opposing views, often the way with academics. Neither could agree, for example, on **why** Danny Boyle, the writer, producer and director had given the actor playing Isambard Kingdom Brunel (one of the Victorian gentlemen who had descended from the carriage), a speech from *The Tempest* to proclaim. It began:

Be not afeard; the isle is full of noises,

Sounds and sweet airs, that give delight, and hurt not.

Jo wasn't sure she cared why, she just found herself remembering the first line so that when the waves of drummers came on beating an incessant rhythm the words 'Be not afeard' echoed on in her head with the drum beats.

'You're enjoying the drums, aren't you Jo,' said Grandma, giving her a wink. She knew full well that although Jo's mother was proud of her daughter's drumming ability, she would have much preferred her to have taken up an instrument such as the flute or the oboe, and to have played classical music rather than the rock sounds made by Jo and the others in her band.

'I am, Grandma, I am; the sound so expresses the industrial activity… ooh, look at that!' Jo, like everyone else was suddenly lost for words as there appeared to be a river of molten metal flowing round the stadium into huge rings of fire – rings of fire that, before their eyes, turned into a burning symbol hung in the sky of the six continents of the world – the Olympic rings.

Later that evening Jo and Alex received a formal message from SHARP. The voice at the other end of the phone was not one either of them recognized and told them that they were both able to listen at the same time and respond if they wanted to.

'Welcome both of you to a new MISSION. Alex, this is the first time you have a worked as a full agent for us. Previously you have been with the organisation known as STRAP. We hope you are convinced by what our agent, Danny Higgins, has told you with regard to the unreliability of that organisation. We will be sending you our usual information about our methods but Jo has no need of them so that will be done later. You can both reply to us as you read this message if you need to.

We have just watched a ceremony that relied on, amongst other things, huge amounts of forward planning, precision timing, and the full co-operation of all who took part. What we are proposing to do now also relies on those things. We are currently in the stage of forward-planning and we are making good progress. Our deadline date in the past is 29th June 1613, that is 400 years plus 1 month back in time from now. You possibly do not know what happened on 29th June 1613 – it is the date that the first Globe theatre was destroyed by fire.

We are proposing to synchronise the sending of you both back to the same place and same date. In order to achieve this we will need precision timing. This precision timing is made easier if both of you are in the same place and, of course, the same time. Jo is going to visit her grandma in Brighton. You too, Alex, will be in Brighton.'

At this point Alex spluttered, 'But…I live in Edinburgh.'

'Of course, we know that, but don't worry. It is almost certainly set up for you to be in Brighton in time for this joint MISSION.

Unlike the other trips in which you have been involved, we are hoping that ,on this occasion, you will uncover the truth about an historic event. If we know the truth about this event, it will make a huge difference to our being able to track the traces of destruction from that time forward to your present day. For this reason we are expending a large amount of our resources on this MISSION and so, we are relying on your complete co-operation. Do we have your co-operation?'

Jo and Alex both replied with the one word: 'Yes'.

'Your contact person for this mission for both of you will

be Kazeresh Porterman who you, Alex, know as Kaz. He is more experienced than Mela, with whom Jo is generally in contact. He will keep a very careful eye on all data so as to ensure your safe arrival and return. We will get back to you.'

The transmission stopped abruptly.

Jo reached for her phone to contact Alex, but he was there before her, and it was her phone that buzzed.

'Wow, this is something, isn't it,' said Alex.

'Yes, going back to the night the Globe burnt down is an amazing thought. But, it does sound dangerous.'

'It does. We had better read up all we can find about it.'

'I've already done that, as part of our school Elizabethan end of term stuff. There's not a lot on the internet really and some of it is contradictory.'

'Perhaps that's what all this is about. It sounds like we are going to be doing some sleuthing.'

'Yes, but…'

'You don't sound too keen.'

'Well, honestly Alex, I'm not the bravest of people. I didn't tell you but when I went back to Stratford

I got some awful Elizabethan bug, it might have been smallpox.'

'OMG, that does sound scary.'

'SHARP used their advanced technology and zapped it, but it did make me worry about safety and stuff, and I am especially afraid of fire.'

'Well, I've never given it much thought, to be honest, but yes I suppose fire is scary.'

'I am petrified of fire.'

'Don't worry, they'll give the dangerous stuff to me – that's probably why I've been drafted in, while you can do the intellectual stuff.'

'I wouldn't want you being exposed to danger, either. But, don't get the wrong idea, I'm not about to pull out. No way. '

'Great. I think we'll make good partners.'

'Same here, speak to you soon, Alex.'

'Cheers, Jo.'

CHAPTER 9

The Blind Tiger Club

Between the 28th July and the 10th August 2012 the following text messages and phone calls were exchanged by Jo Kelly and Alex McLean.

They were all intercepted and monitored by the organisation from the future called SHARP.

Alex: Jo, I've been selected to climb for my club team but guess what? The first contest is against some small club down south. It's the Adur Centre in Hove near Brighton!"!!!!! We climb there on Wed 8th August. Mum and Dad are thinking of making it a week's holiday!

Sent: 28 Jul

Jo: Huge congrats on your selection Alex. You must be a really good climber. Obviously SHARP knew your club was planning this contest. You'll be in Brighton before me. We are arriving Fri 10th August. Let me know how you get on in the contest.

Sent: 28 Jul

Alex: I've been on Wiki about the fire. Seems that everyone got out alive. So no worries.

Sent: 2 Aug

Jo: That's for the people who were supposed to be there. It doesn't cover people from another time. And, their news reporting was sketchy in those days. I'm not worrying about the fire... well I'm trying not to. Mum and Dad taking us out for meals to make up for being away. Gran has gone back to Brighton. Have you told your girlfriend about your selection to the club team?

Sent: 2 Aug

Alex: No, I've told you instead. I've had loads of company instructions from SHARP all about their systems of working and policy for ensuring we are safe and so on. They are going to supply us with something that fits into your ear, apparently it's really tiny and translates Elizabethan English into present day.

Sent: 2 Aug

Jo: I had one of those before. They work well. The time is going by soooo slowly. Even my friends, Emily and Ruby, are moaning about it. They can't wait to get to Brighton. I haven't told you but they are coming to stay with me at my grandma's house in Brighton for a few days and visit this fabulous place called 'The Blind Tiger' where young musicians can perform. Oh and I've not explained to you that we have our own band: Emily sings, Ruby plays keyboard and I'm on drums. There's a guy called Stuart who's in our band as well and he was going to come to Brighton but he can't now.

Sent: 2 Aug

Alex: Wow your band stuff is really cool.

Sent: 2 Aug

Jo: We've played for school and stuff in Oxford but apparently there is this jam session for young bands at 'The Blind Tiger' club and we might be able to play. I am not sure which I'm more excited about – time travel or going to the CLUB!

Sent: 3 Aug

Alex: I bet. What day is that on?

Sent: 3 Aug

Jo: Sat 11th August. It starts at 2pm and finishes 5pm. I do hope you can come.

Sent: 5 Aug

Alex: Jo, I've just worked out that I have got to be there. Think about it: You are not getting to Brighton until Friday. You are going to this place 'The Blind Tiger' on the Saturday, Dad's booked a hotel Sunday to Sunday. The only one time we can be together in the same place is at this club!

Sent: 10 Aug

Jo: You're right, but how on earth is that going to work? I'll be with two friends and the place will be packed.

Sent: 10 Aug

Alex: We'll have to wait and see.

Sent: 10 Aug

In the next few days, both Alex and Jo received instructions from SHARP that gave them the date, June 1613, and where they would be landing. Alex would be landing outside the Tower of London and Jo in the church called St. Mary Overy, which later was called Southwark Cathedral . The instructions then went on to give them much more detail than usual. They were told, among other things, what clothes to wear, and how and when to communicate to each other.

Alex was told that he should make his way from the Tower to the Globe in time for the afternoon's performance of the play now called 'Henry the Eighth' but which was then called 'All is True'. He was to keep his mobile in the time/space travel bag as usual.

Jo was told that she would arrive early in the morning, and that she would find a basket at the church which she must take with her. Inside her time/space travel bag, she would find a small purse to wear on her wrist that had money in it so that she could buy food on her way to the Globe theatre for the actors to eat before their performance. She was told to put her mobile in that bag and not take the time/space travel bag with her.

It was clear that SHARP were very serious about trying to pinpoint how the fire at the Globe had started.

The only thing they didn't make clear was where Jo and Alex would meet in Brighton so as to carry out the instructions. 'Prepare and leave at the same place and the same time', was all that they said, as if it was the easiest thing in the world for young teenagers to avoid parents, friends and grandparents to meet up. So Jo and Alex agreed that they were right in assuming that 'The Blind Tiger' would have to be their meeting place.

Alex was in Brighton by Sunday, 5th August. In the days before Jo was due to arrive, he and his mum and dad explored the beach, the pier, the old town with its maze of streets called 'the Lanes,' and, of course, the Brighton Pavilion. Alex met up with his teammates from the Edinburgh climbing club for a practice session at the Adur Outdoor Activities Centre in Hove, and then on the Wednesday took part in the climbing contest, which the Edinburgh team won.

Alex googled 'The Blind Tiger Club' and found that it was about half a mile from their hotel, so on Saturday morning, after a very leisurely breakfast (while Maureen and Jock were shuffling through brochures to decide what place to visit for their last day in Brighton) Alex was concentrating on plans to avoid going with them.

'Look, Mum, what great stuff they have going on in Brighton for teens. We've nothing like this in Edinburgh!' Alex held out a folded over page from a local newspaper in front of his mum. Maureen read it through and looked puzzled.

'Since when have you been interested in this kind of music, Alex?' She passed the paper to Jock.

Jock read out the first two lines of the article: '...*Calling all fans! Young up-and-coming punk rock band, A-M-I (short for Anti Meathead Inc), are hosting a club session at The Blind Tiger, Saturday 11th August! A must for all teens who follow the new sounds coming from Brighton's music scene. Meet two punk-rock legends, Charlie Harper of U.K. Subs and Captain Sensible of the Damned, both backing this new venture!*' Jock paused and looked at his wife. 'Well, Maureen, I can understand Alex wanting to go along to see punk rock legend Captain Sensible – wouldn't mind going myself. You know I used to be a fan of punk music.'

Alex drew in a quick breath – Oh no, not his mum and dad coming too! He needn't have worried. Maureen was having none of it. She insisted on a visit to some haunted mansion on the outskirts of Brighton, while Jock reluctantly agreed that his punk-rocker days were over and, although he could remember the two 'legends' mentioned in the article he could only remember one song, *Emotional Blackmail* that he thought had been a hit for one or other of them.

After a lot of negotiating, Maureen finally agreed, Alex could go to the gig at The Blind Tiger if he wanted to, but she insisted on lunch first and that Alex must be back at the hotel by 6 o'clock. By the time lunch was finished, the afternoon session at The Blind Tiger had started, and even though Alex sprinted most of the way from the hotel to the club, he still arrived late.

As he squeezed into the crowd of teenagers, phones held above their heads and eyes glued to the figure on the stage, he realized he had arrived just in time to hear Charlie Harper, a really cool looking guy with truly spectacular tattoos, perform with the young band A-M-I. It was awesome. The music thumped into his head and seemed to extract all thoughts, even those of time travel. But at some point, he realised that the number they were performing was the one his dad had remembered: *Emotional Blackmail.*

When it finished the whoops, calls and stamping of feet mingled with feverish applause. But then there was a bit of a lull with the usual band stuff, fiddling with electronics and general chat before a very young guy called Javi got up to introduce his group. 'We're the grasshopper with a small g,' he smiled, and again the crowd clapped enthusiastically. Fortunately, this group, although still loud, was a bit quieter than A-M-I and Alex had managed to call Jo to tell her that he was at the back of the club. Jo had no trouble slipping away from her friends – they were completely gone with the scene. She spotted Alex hovering at the back.

'Did you hear us perform?' Jo asked, her cheeks red with the excitement of it, 'They let us have a spot on the open jam session it was fantastic – Emily did really well!'

'I'm so sorry, but I missed it. I had quite a lot of trouble getting away from Mum and Dad.'

'I expect you did, but what on earth are we going to do now?'

'We've got to find somewhere in the building that isn't being used. Come on.' Alex headed pushed open the door. They tried the toilets, but there were far too many kids in there, and then they spotted a small corridor. It was empty of people. They tried a couple of doors but they were locked… and then, one opened. It was a small room for the cleaners with buckets, mops and brushes. They nodded quickly to each other and then nipped inside, closing the door behind them.

'I've got my costume in my backpack,' said Jo starting to change and Alex got out of most of his clothes, which he stuffed into the top of Jo's backpack. Alex had his time/space bag which had already been delivered to his hotel room that morning in the usual mysterious SHARP way. He stuck it to the side of his stomach where it stuck securely. Jo had the small Elizabethan purse that dangled at her wrist. Both extracted the translator aid and slipped it into one ear. Then, Jo counted '1…2…3' and they both dialed the project number in perfect synchronization. The high pitched whine came with alarming speed and ferocity. Then… Nothing.

CHAPTER 10

One Destination –
Shakespeare's Globe

JO'S ARRIVAL IN LONDON, 1613

There was a hard, stone floor underneath Jo's feet. When she opened her eyes, the light that filtered through the thickly-leaded windows was only just enough for her to make out thick, stone pillars towering one after the other down the long nave. But one determined ray of sunlight struck through a small pane of glass and lit up, as if with fire, the gold cross on the altar. For a while, Jo could not take her eyes off it; yes she was definitely in a church, quite a large church.

Glad to feel clear-headed, for once, after arriving back in time, she could remember all the complicated instructions she had been given. This was the Year 1613 and she was in London, presumably in the church called St Mary Overy. She quickly slipped the camera disc out of the time/space bag and pressed it to her forehead until the film came away and dissolved into her skin. She put the backing in the bag and remembered that she had to keep her mobile in the little purse dangling from her wrist.

Now to look for the basket, she thought. She scanned around but could see no sign of a basket. Then, from one side of the church, a door opened and small woman, bent over with age and dressed in black, from the shawl wound round her head to her feet, shuffled towards her.

'Have you come to pray young Mistress?' asked the old woman, her voice not much more than a whisper.

'I…I have prayed this morning in my house,' Jo lied convincingly.

'Then why are you here young Mistress?'

'I've come to look for a basket,' Jo said, unable to think of anything but the truth to say this time.

The old woman straightened up a little. 'Ah, it was you that forgot their belongings, was it?' the old woman's voice was reprimanding now, no longer a frail whisper. She wagged a stern finger at Jo. 'In my day, young people were taught to take care of the things they had, but not nowadays. Ways have changed – all is slapdash now! I know not what the world is coming to.'

She ranted on for quite some time, during which Jo was having trouble trying not to grin; clearly that would never get the old bag to give up what presumably someone had left behind on their last visit to St Mary Overy.

Then, abruptly, the old woman turned and, much more quickly than before, scuttled back to the door out of which she had come. A few moments later, she came back with a basket which, Jo noticed, looked very like the one she had had before in Stratford. The old woman held it out towards her, somewhat reluctantly, and then it occurred to Jo: the reason for the old woman's grumpiness might have been because she had hoped to keep the basket for herself.

'I must take the basket now, but I won't be needing it at all after today. Would you like me to bring it back here?' Jo asked helpfully.

The old woman's expression changed to one of righteous piety. 'It is good to give to our Lord,' she said, 'and what you give to those who look after his house, is giving to him.'

Once again, Jo stifled a chuckle, what an old hypocrite!

Once outside, after the quiet of the church, noise hit Jo like a violent assault as she made her way along a small rutted roadway. Although early in the morning, people were milling about all around her, men pushing handcarts, calling out to each other or to the occupants of the nearby houses, women with baskets, some laden already with shopping, chattering at full volume or shouting at the children scampering along beside them. A horse rider or two would clop by and the wheels of carts pulled by small stocky horses passed perilously close to Jo's feet. Above it all, large, black birds circled rhythmically, swooping down to snatch up something for their breakfast from a pile of garbage at the side of the road. Jo could hear the harsh squawk of gulls, coming from the river, the same sound that greeted her in the early morning at her grandma's home in Brighton. What survivors those gulls are, she thought.

Worried at first about how to buy the food she was supposed to get, Jo actually found it surprisingly easy. By following the women with empty baskets, she soon came upon a small roadside market selling bread, cooked meat, fruit and vegetables. All she had to do was take one of the coins from the purse, point to whatever it was she wanted, take it with a quiet 'thank you,' and keep her hand out for the change; there always seemed to be change so she assumed there was plenty of money in her purse.

With her basket full, Jo made her way towards the Globe. She thought this would be easy because the outline of the almost circular theatre could be clearly seen above the roofs of the modest houses. However, the small narrow streets, sometimes with houses on and sometimes bordered by bushes, were not being very helpful. Just as the walls of the Globe seemed to be almost at touching distance, the road would bend away and her path would be blocked by other buildings. At one point, she found herself back outside St Mary's church. She was beginning to feel very frustrated and worried that, at such an early stage, she was failing. She set off once more, but this time, she became aware that a small boy was following her. Maybe he had spotted that she was a newcomer to the district and thought she would be an easy prey for a pickpocket. She listened to his footfalls, tracking hers, then suddenly spun round to face him.

'Are you following me?' she asked, frowning and looking him up and down sternly. He was much too small to be a vicious assailant, no more than seven or eight years old, she thought.

'I meant n…no harm, young Mistress, honest.'

'Well, were you following me?'

'You look like you might be lost,' he said.

'And that's a reason to…to set upon me?'

'Truly, truly, I meant no harm,' he brushed a very grubby hand across his eyes.

'Well, I'm still waiting for answer; were you following me?'

'Yes, I…I thought I might help you and then you might…might give me, give me a penny…or so.'

He looked so small and downcast, and, Jo realised, so terribly hungry.'

'You are right, right on two matters. Firstly I am lost and secondly if you can help me, I will certainly give you a penny…or maybe even two.'

A heart-breaking smile spread across his face.

'Where is it you want to go? Is it over the river to Cheapside?'

'No, no, I want to go to the Globe Theatre.'

His face looked astonished. 'Why, it is just there,' and he pointed to the roof of the Globe that was easily seen above the houses.

'I know, but every time I get near to it, the street bends away and takes me back the way the way I've come.'

'Oh, that's because you've missed the back alley. Come on we'll be there in a trice.' A small grubby hand took hold of Jo's and a few minutes later they were squeezing down the narrowest of spaces between houses and then coming out on a broader roadway right beside the theatre. 'You should have took the road by the Thames and not gone up so far to the church,' he said glowing with pride at his London knowledge.

Jo extracted two coins from the purse and put them in his hand.

He handed one back, shaking his head, 'That was such a small help,' he said, 'I can't take that much from you.'

'Yes you can,' said Jo, buy yourself some food, and some for…' she was going to say 'your mother' but then worried that maybe he didn't have one. 'Some for…'

'My Annie?'

'Yes for your Annie. And now just show me the door that will take me into the theatre where I can find the actors, for I have brought this basket of food for them.'

'Master William Shakespeare always looks after the actors that put on his plays. He is the best of men and the best of playwrights.'

Jo was taken aback at this accolade for Shakespeare from such an unlikely source. 'Yes I quite agree with you there, but aren't you a bit young to know whether he is the best of playwrights or not? Surely you are too young to watch the plays of such a playwright?'

The boy shook his head.

'I would watch all day if I could, but sometimes I'm not allowed.' He was backing away from her as he spoke.

Suddenly, on an impulse, Jo said, 'And what's your name, young fan of William Shakespeare?'

'Stephen, 'cos I was born on the Saint's day in December. ' The boy turned quickly and ran off back into the maze of streets from which they had just emerged.

ALEX'S ARRIVAL IN LONDON, 1613

It was hardly light when Alex opened his eyes. He was stretched out on a rough, wooden bench, his head pillowed on a heap of ragged clothes, a rough cloth cape over him. He sat up slowly to allow the unpleasant throbbing sensation in his head to subside. He scanned the wide open space around him and saw that where he was, there were other bodies lying about, seemingly asleep. Clearly this was a spot for those who had no home to go to.

As his brain cleared, it dawned on him that maybe he might not have far to look for his Elizabethan clothes. Yes – his crude pillow was made up of some plain, not very clean, items of clothing, which he hastily put on in case any of the sleeping bodies woke up. There were brown breeches coming to his knees and a shirt, that maybe had once been white, that had no collar, but two ties to pull together round his neck. There was also a little jacket with no sleeves that was made of something quite thick; obviously the clothes of a working lad. He put the camera disc on his forehead, waiting for the film to dissolve into his skin and slipped his phone into the time/space bag that was sticking, as ever, firmly and smoothly to his stomach. He hitched the breeches up over to make sure the time/space bag was securely hidden. They came up quite high, like Simon Cowell trousers, he thought, smiling at the ridiculous comparison.

He looked around at the wider view. How strange, he had only been to London the once on the school trip and yet, he knew where he was, without a doubt. Behind him, four-square and solid, was the unmistakable stone block of the Tower of London. He could tell that there were a few differences, but they were negligible. The Norman conqueror had built a castle fortification that had brooded over London for centuries and would survive even more centuries when other famous London landmarks would succumb to flames, German bombers, or the dreaded bulldozer.

He sat for a while, thinking what he should do next. For some reason, although SHARP had given him such precise instructions of how to work with Jo, they had not explained to him why he was arriving at this early time of the day. He had got quite a way to walk to get to the Globe. And then another thought came to him. Money? He would need money to get into the Globe. He felt down the sides of the breeches, no pockets, and there were certainly no pockets in the jacket. Had there been a coin left with the clothes which he had not spotted? There was nothing on the bench and nothing under it. How did SHARP think he was going to get into the theatre? He remembered distinctly the tour guide informing them that those who watched the play standing, the ones called the groundlings, paid a penny to get in. He hadn't got that penny. Was he supposed to try to bluff his way in? Surely, the Elizabethan ticket collectors would be well on top of such a move.

Just then, a racket started up as several hand

carts pulled onto the space in front of the Tower. Where before there were sleeping bodies, now the clatter of horses hooves, and various shouts and 'ahoys' woke everyone. Alex noticed that most of the sleeping bodies had been boys, much about his age and that they started to approach the men with horse-drawn and hand-drawn carts, obviously angling for work. The street merchants began setting out their wares on the carts, transforming the space into a market. A street trader with a small horse-drawn cart drew up within inches of Alex's feet.

'Well done, boy. You've saved my pitch!' A heavy hand landed on Alex's shoulder and a broad, chubby bloke with the most awful black teeth dug him in the ribs. 'Did you give Charlie a fight for the privilege of helping me out, or has he got himself a more advantageous situation?'

Alex shrugged, 'It's just for the day, sir, I think he had some…some business he had to attend to.'

'Well then, let's get busy before the ladies get here.' The man let down one of the sides of the cart and propped it up to make a wide flat surface on which to display his goods. He motioned towards Alex to get on the cart and pass forward various bags, which he singled out by pointing his stubby forefinger at them. His goods turned out to be mostly vegetables, of which turnips in various sizes and colours were the most numerous. There were also a lot of bunches of green stuff that Alex couldn't identify, probably different kinds of herbs. Following the traders instructions he arranged them in a pile at the front of the stall. Most of these gave off a pungent smell – a welcome change to the other smells that assaulted Alex's nose. The day was warming up and Alex began to break out into a sweat. When the goods were all displayed, the man handed him a pile of hay. Alex stood holding it like an idiot. The man tipped his hat and scratched his head.

'You're a strange 'un, who do you think that's for? It's not for you – it's for him.' He pointed at the horse which still stood patiently between the shafts of the cart.

Of course, thought Alex, the horse. He dropped the pile of hay just below the horse's nose and it was clearly expecting its meal, as it started munching straight away.

'And now your hay, young man,' said his employer slapping a thigh and laughing at his joke. He passed Alex a couple of coins which Alex gratefully took.

'There'll be more for you if you are back to help me pack up,'

'Well sir... I need to get to the Globe Theatre, sir, on the south of the Thames. Can you direct me?'

'So you're one of those deep country lads? Hopin' to get work as a lass are ye?'

He let out a loud guffaw.

'No, indeed...Sir. I just want to *watch* the play.' The trader looked at him puzzled. Something did not quite fit...the way he spoke...? But, the lad had been a good help, what matter where he was from?

'Well boy. The cheapest seats are the best, cost just one penny. You're thin enough to slip through the other penny stinkards to the edge of the stage. Enjoy the play and if you're back in time, you can tell me all about it. Be on your way – through that lane is the quickest to London Bridge.' The stubby finger now pointed to a road that looked little more than an alley-way between two houses.

'Thank you, sir.' Alex began to walk away. 'I'll do my very best to get back in time for your packing up... I don't know what might happen though,' Alex added, more to himself than to the trader.

'Count the heads on the way!' the man called after him.

What did he mean by that?

Alex found out when he got to the other side of London Bridge, although getting to the other side was not the easiest thing in the world. No, he was not about to take lovely bracing stroll through a city. He was, in fact, about to navigate narrow streets, polluted with rubbish and with the contents of chamber pots swilling down the middle. What a dirty lot these people are, thought Alex. Clearly, caring for the environment hadn't entered their heads.

It was fortunate that when Alex began to get near to the bridge, the houses thinned out, probably because of the boggy land sloping down towards the Thames. He could see the stretch of river clearly and the many broad, stone arches spanning the wide expanse of water. Surely the river was much wider than it was in the twenty-first century? Here on the north bank, the wind had picked up and river smells overpowered the dreadful ones that Alex had had to endure in the streets, but even so, it didn't smell too good! Mud, salt water and sewage. What really amazed him, though, was that all the way across the bridge there were buildings, and even a small church.

When he got onto the roadway on the bridge, he found that it was packed with traffic, horses, carts, and people going in both directions, north and south. Alex pressed forward as best he could. He began to worry about whether he would make it to the Globe in time. Then he began to realise that a lot of the people crossing the bridge were, like him, intending to go the Globe for that afternoon's performance. In Elizabethan times, nobody seemed to talk quietly. Their conversations were loud, raucous and unselfconsciously shared with anyone else who was nearby. So when Alex found himself following behind three men whose garments where much finer than those of most of the other people around him, he could follow their conversation easily. They obviously knew a lot about Shakespeare, perhaps they even knew him.

After discussing the merits of the last play of his they had seen, *The Tempest*, they started to be quite derogatory about a play called, '*About Our Time*', the one that was on that afternoon, Alex found himself listening in on the conversation.

'Well we shall see if their much-vaunted spectaculars come up to standards this afternoon, will we not?' A great deal of laughter followed this remark and Alex wondered why, for there had been nothing very funny about the words.

'Oh I think the spectacle will outdo anything that

has been seen before on Will Shakespeare's precious stage up to this very day!' The sarcasm and, yes, hostility, was unmistakable this time. Alex got as close to the men as he dared because suddenly they had lowered their voices, as if worried they might be overheard. Then,to Alex's dismay, one swung round and looked straight at him, but Alex needn't have worried; he looked straight through him as if he didn't exist – obviously a working boy was of no interest or consequence. He turned back to talk to the other men, but Alex had had a good look at his handsome face and fine clothes, but most of all he noticed his hat adorned with the blue-green eyes of a clutch of curling peacock feathers.

'They have the cannon ready to be pulled out onto the stage, I believe. My sources inform me it is their usual trusty man, John Smith, who has the job of firing, he never misses but 'miss' he will today. That is according 'to all accounts' and those accounts are ones that we will be putting out. You can be sure, none of the rest of the audience will have the slightest notion of what actually happened.'

'No there'll be too busy gawping at the stage,' agreed one.

'And I am certain that, H.W. will confirm our accounts to those to whom he writes – that it was the firing of the canon that caused the little disaster at Master Shakespeare's theatre. My good friend Sir H.W. believes every word I utter.' There followed more laughter. The more he heard, the more suspicious Alex became; these men's innuendos clearly had some malice in them.

'One thing we must be sure of doing is leaving the theatre as soon as…' Alex had to wait then for a few seconds as a carriage came by on the other side and the men got ahead of him. It was near the end of the bridge and Alex attention was suddenly diverted by a gruesome sight.

'Count the heads,' the trader had called out after him, and there – stuck up on poles at the top of the south gate were the severed heads of traitors; deep eye-sockets and gaping mouths sending a horrible shudder down the spine. They were not yet white skulls because black pitch was preserving them in what was obviously thought to be eternal damnation.

CHAPTER 11

Inside The Globe Again

Jo stood motionless inside the quiet theatre. It was true! The theatre she had been in with her school, the new Globe in London, was an exact replica of this, the original theatre built by Shakespeare and his friends. Everything was the same, the pillars, the balconies, the tiered benches, the apron stage with its heavy red curtain at the back – all exactly the same. There was a difference, though. The one she was standing in now was shabbier, more scuffed, more well-used ; you could say, in serious need of a coat of modern-day paint.

Walking forward into the groundlings' space, Jo became aware of two people pacing up and down on the stage. They were muttering to themselves. Then one stopped.

'I think I've got it!' he shouted. 'I've got it at last, Tom. Let's try that scene again.'

The one called Tom moved to the centre of the stage and began his lines in a commanding voice that projected right to the back of the theatre, no way did he need a microphone. Then he spotted Jo and stopped in full flow. He let out a kind of whoop and beckoned Jo forward onto the stage.

'Hey everyone, the food's arrived!' The next minute, she was surrounded by five or six young men eager to get their hands in the basket.

'Hang on, you lot. This has got to be shared out fairly,' said the first actor, who seemed to be the one in charge. 'Don't knock the poor girl over.' He came and relieved Jo of the basket, at which point everyone's attention turned to the contents of the basket and no one took any notice of Jo at all. She had little trouble in slipping behind the thick curtain at the back of the stage and into the room behind.

'Wooo,' she whispered.

She was in a space crammed from corner to corner with costumes and all manner of props, most notably of which was a rack of various types of weapons from tall staves and pikes to bright shining, curved swords, everything you could use to slice, chop or spear a person.

But she mustn't linger. She mustn't let curiosity win over fear. She was backstage and in with a chance. She mustn't blow it. If anyone came in, they would definitely throw her out. She had to be quick and get up onto the next floor, but where were the stairs? It was gloomy and dark, and the piles of clothes and clutter made it hard to see. Against the back wall, there were several suits of armour. When Jo looked carefully she saw, thankfully, that one of the suits of armour obscured a flight of stairs, not much more than a ladder really.

The room on the second floor was arranged much more tidily, helped by a good amount of light coming through the windows that looked out on to the stage below. This room was also full of costumes and Jo could see that these were mainly for women, long brocade dresses, under skirts, ruffs and black bodices, all hung up neatly on rails. There were others, loose flowing garments, were they for the Roman ladies in Anthony and Cleopatra? And strange black gowns with torn ragged edges, perhaps for the witches in Macbeth? Despite knowing she was still in danger of discovery, Jo couldn't resist looking around. It was so fascinating. There was a table with make-up, pots of powder and red and brown pastes, a tumble of wigs in a box, and in one corner, a table with a pile of papers.

She should be going up to the next floor, but the sound of voices coming from the stairs warned her that she had no time to do that. All she had time to do, was to clamber into a cupboard at the back of the room and squeeze herself into a dusty space between the skirts hanging from the rail above. The people who had come into the room turned out to be three extremely noisy lads of around fourteen or fifteen years old, who with great fuss and to-do proceeded to make themselves up into court ladies with under-skirts, top skirts, sleeves, bodices, ruffs, wigs and last of all a lot make-up. They took a great deal of time over their make-up and Jo, who had quite a good view of this, had a huge difficulty stifling giggles that threatened to explode her out of the cupboard.

At last they were gone and Jo was able to make her way up to the attic floor where she had been told to hide. Once again, there were many possible hiding places and this time, she chose one carefully. It was a long, low wooden box with nothing much in it but a few ropes. There were a lot of other ropes around in this space. She wasn't too sure what they were for, but then she saw what looked like trap doors in the floor, and she wondered if the ropes were used for actors to swing down onto the stage, as if from the heavens above.

Before creeping into her hiding place, Jo had a look through the small attic window. Down below, people were beginning to fill up the seats and the standing only area around the stage. She watched for a while hoping to see Alex, but she couldn't. What if he wasn't there? What if she was on her own? For a moment she stood unable to move by the window.

The thought of the fire began to stifle out any others. Fire, with its black poisonous smoke, suffocating her and flames licking at her flesh. Whether criminals started the fire, as SHARP seemed convinced about, or whether it was in fact the cannon that set light to the thatch, as the historians believed, hardly mattered to her now. What mattered was her fear, fear that she would be engulfed by flames. Would SHARP be able to save her then? She cowered down in her box and was on the point of pressing the red emergency button to take her back to safety in the twenty-first century when a text came in.

I'm in the theatre, not long now, don't worry, you'll be alright.

Jo looked at the words and her spirits lifted a little. The text stayed on the screen for moment and then disappeared leaving the screen blank with just the three phoenix icons. At least Alex was here and she was not alone.

Alex had maneuvered himself to just two rows from the stage. The crowd around him was made up of people of all ages, excited, noisy and happy. When he had settled into his space, he noticed a family group of three generations immediately in front of him. He did a mental summary of their roles. That jolly one's the mother; the older woman, almost as excited, has got to be her mother and the grandmother of those three under ten-year-old kids and that boy, who is about my age, maybe? The burly man must be the husband engrossed in recounting some recent event with the old, grisly man, the grandfather. By the sound of things, he is gloating over winning a bet on cockfighting at a nearby site and his winnings are paying for this visit to the Globe. What a strange world!

Following SHARP's instructions, he had to send a text message to Jo to let her know he was in the theatre. He managed to dig his phone out from the securely fastened bag under his shirt while the family in front of him started unpacking what looked like a picnic. The mother had placed a linen cloth at the edge of stage and chunks of bread, meat and cheese so that the family could all help themselves. It kept them fully engrossed so Alex felt sure they would not notice the strange apparatus in his hand as he quickly typed a message to Jo.

The one that came back from her said:

Thanks, I'm in the attic. I'm in a chest and I've propped open the lid with a small piece of rope. Can just see out through the crack.

Alex felt worried. Why, he wondered, had SHARP given Jo such a dangerous part of their mission? Surely they knew she was horribly scared of fire? She was a great kid; he wouldn't for a minute suggest that girls would be more scared then boys, but what if Jo had a panic attack she couldn't control?

Just then there was a flurry of extra excitement as some musicians came out onto the stage to entertain the audience with dancing and singing before the play. These jolly entertainers were not at all put off by the noise from the audience. Each time they stopped for a breather, the audience cheered and shouted encouragement.

Alex noticed that the groundlings' space had filled up first, now all the balconies were filling up too. He looked intently at all of those occupying, what he judged to be, the best seats in the house and was sure that he spotted the group of three suspicious characters that he had followed on the way to the theatre. Yes, sure enough there was the man with peacock feathers in his hat. He must keep his eyes on them once the play started.

Then a buzz went round the whole theatre as a huge iron cannon was pushed and pulled on to the stage by four sweating stage hands. After that, it was clear that the play was about to start. In pairs, actors and musicians, vigorously striking out their tunes, entered from behind the curtain. They fanned out to the edges of the stage, then froze into a pose suitable to the part they were soon to play. All the cast, barring King Henry VIII, were now on the stage.

With some pomp and pageantry, the actor who was to speak the prologue stepped centre stage to the sound of drum rolls. He stopped within a pace or two of the groundlings. Side or centre, the actors were all dressed in fine clothes fit for a royal play. The members of the audience silenced their chat, shushed their children and soon an intense hush fell over the theatre.

Alex could see that all, even the small children, had their gaze fixed intently on the actor. With great earnestness the actor playing the prologue delivered his warning to the audience:

> 'I come no more to make you laugh: things now,
> That bear a weighty and a serious brow,
> Sad, high, and working, full of state and woe,
> Such noble scenes as draw the eye to flow,
> We now present. Those that can pity, here
> May, if they think it well, let fall a tear…'

When he had finished, he bowed low with a great flourish of his feathered hat, and retired to the side of the stage. The play began.

CHAPTER 12

Fire!

It was hard for Alex to follow the action of the play as all his concentration was focused on watching for the moment the cannon was to be discharged. He knew that it was to be let off to signal the entry of King Henry the Eighth. The moment was nearly upon them, and while everyone else faced the stage, Alex swiveled round and intently watched the thatched roof opposite the stage, and the patch of sky above it. And sure enough, as the cannon exploded and the audience cheered, he saw that the ball of wadding flew over the roof as intended. Smothering, white smoke mushroomed from the end of the cannon making those near the front cough, and the air smelt strongly of fireworks. But Alex had clearly seen that nothing had landed on the roof, although bits of burnt paper and detritus fluttered over the groundlings, some of it caught in an upward draught of air but all of it eventually came down, harmlessly, amongst the laughing crowd, none of whom seemed to mind brushing cinders off their clothes. Alex scanned the audience in the balcony seats and spotted the three shifty men, including the man in the peacock-feathered hat, get up and sidle out of their seats.

A text message came in. Surreptitiously he looked down at his phone. Jo's text said simply.

A rough looking man is setting fire to the thatch in the attic with a burning torch!

This is it, thought Alex. This is when things start to get dangerous, especially for Jo!

He looked up and thought he saw a slight glow behind the window, but then it went out. He kept watching the window and the roof above it. At first there seemed nothing to get alarmed about but then a small wisp of smoke came smoldering and twisting up through the thatch, starting to spiral along the upper section of the roof.

As yet, no one in the audience and none of the actors appeared to have noticed. He felt a jab of fear tighten in his throat. He sent Jo a text:

Have you got out of there yet?

I can't the man's still here. He is talking to another man,

one dressed much more finely. The man in fine clothes is handing him money.

A man with fine clothes? Alex suddenly latched on to the message Jo had sent.

Quick Jo, can you describe what he's wearing, especially his hat.

Yellow tights, black puffy breeches cape red mostly hat with peacock feathers.

Thanks, I'll tell you why when I see you. Get out NOW.

There was no reply from Jo, so Alex assumed she was fleeing from the attic. If she went down the stairs straight away, she would be outside the Globe pretty quickly.

But Jo wasn't out of the attic yet. The man who had set fire to the thatch had left but then came back in. He was looking for something on the floor. Jo was still cowering in the wooden chest, her heart pounding so loudly she thought he might hear it as he bent down to pick up – a long-bladed, wicked-looking knife.

The play was in full swing now, with all kinds of dramatic exits and entrances. The crowds booed a character they didn't like and clapped and cheered another that they did.

Alex watched the smoke starting to thicken. Why had no one else noticed? He shook the arm of the man in front of him, the father of the family who had so enjoyed their meal.

'Look, look, smoke coming from the roof, can't you see?'

'Aye you're right,' said the man. 'Could be, it's another of the clever effects the King's Men are so good at.'

'No, look it's worse than that.' Alex tried to get his attention properly.

The man seemed slightly dazed and tapped his wife on the shoulder. She looked up, and the smile on her face began to darken as the man spoke to her and turned to include the others in their party. All of this seemed to be taking a horribly long time. These people didn't seem to have any idea of the seriousness; were they still supposing the drifts of smoke were stage effects? Suddenly, Alex knew why SHARP had put him on the ground floor, maybe he was in the space of some sharp-eyed boy who set off the alarm all those centuries back. Now, one thing was for sure, that's what he had to do.

Alex clambered on the stage and rushed towards the tall actor who had spoken The Prologue. The man made signs at him to get back with an angry frown on his face, obviously thinking he was an idiot trying to gain a moment's glory. Alex grabbed hold of his arm.

'Look! Fire!' Alex shouted. Now the smoke had thickened and small flames were beginning to appear.

The actor, like the family man, looked stunned for a moment, but then took command. He walked centre stage and called out in his strong voice:

'Stop the Play!'

The four actors behind him froze.

'Ladies, gentlemen, please leave your seats. The Globe is on fire! All able-bodied men get to the river with buckets. We actors, with your help, will pour water on the building and put out these flames and save our Globe'. Even at this moment of danger, the man could not stop dramatising.

Alex didn't stop to tell him how futile buckets of water would be. It didn't matter really as long as everyone got out as quickly as they could. He jumped from the stage and started making his way to the exit. He pushed and shoved, no time to be polite or thoughtful. He had to find the man with a peacock feathers in his hat. He was pretty sure the scoundrel would be watching his handiwork somewhere nearby and gloating.

When he got to the exit and pushed his way through the crowds, who were now standing along the embankment of the Thames at a relatively safe distance from the burning building, Alex could feel his temper rising. His fists clenched as he searched the different groups of people. He had to find them, the scoundrels who had done this. He had to confront the peacock man – he was the ring leader he was sure of it. A few people had started to fill buckets with Thames water, but it had soon become pretty obvious that that was useless. The building was now burning strongly from the upper storeys while people were still pouring out of the exits. Blind anger was burning Alex's brain.

Jo had left the attic after the man who had come back for his knife had left the room, and she had now made it to the room below where the women's costumes were stored. A door, she hadn't noticed before, to the left of the stairwell, was half open, leading to the upper balcony – the men must have got out that way.

She turned to look for a moment at the small table in the corner of the room with its pile of papers. The acrid smell of smoke was already filling her nostrils and mouth, fanning the flames of her own personal terror of fire, but on an impulse she moved over to the table. The papers were in a neat pile and tied with a ribbon. On the top piece of paper two words, scrawled in black ink with the 's' shaped like an 'f,' read:

The Tempest

Jo bent down and slowly picked up the bundle papers.

Now full-blown panic was gripping her. Her legs were seizing up, not doing what she was telling them to do, but she made it out of the door and onto the balcony.

A hubbub of people were gesturing and pointing at the flames now firmly taking hold of the thatch. A few of the most elaborately dressed ladies and gentleman were still only just standing up in their seats; others were pushing their way in to join those already making their way along the narrow walkway to the stairwell. Jo joined the people on the walkway. For a few steps she was able to walk at a reasonable pace, but then this changed to a shuffle, a painfully slow shuffle, any faster movement blocked by those in front. Soon, pushed by the press of those behind, she found herself much too close for comfort to the back of a rotund gentleman in a bright yellow brocade jacket, with froths of lace at his neck and sleeves, who kept waving his arms and shouting out, quite uselessly, to those in front to hurry. His hoarse shouting did nothing to speed things up and only seemed to infect others around him, including Jo, with panic. The smoke was thickening.

Gradually, everyone inched towards the first stairwell. But it was at the bottom, when the people from the raised seating on the ground merged with those coming down the stairs, that the crowd became so thick there seemed to be no movement forward at all. That was when full-blown panic gripped Jo. Would they get to the exit in time before flames and smoked engulfed them? Before the flames tasted her skin? A scream welled up in her throat. She tried desperately to hold it in! There was a lot of noise around but no one was screaming yet. Jo was shaking from head to foot, trying to keep a scream from escaping her throat.

Suddenly she became aware that her skirt seemed to catch on a floor board as she inched her way past the now empty tier of seats on the ground floor.

Desperately, she pulled at her skirt. She couldn't move forward! A small space had opened up between her and the fat man in the yellow brocade in front of her. She was being left behind, left behind to burn! She tugged and tugged but it was held fast. Then she bent down to try to unhook it. It was not trapped by a piece of wood but by a small hand! In the space under the tier of benches crouched the small figure of Stephen!

'Stephen, what are you doing there? Come out, you'll burn to death.'

'I've been watching for you, kind and beautiful Mistress. Follow me.'

'Follow you?'

'Yes, I knows a quick way out. I swear. Come, waste no time. Come with me.'

To her own amazement at doing such a thing, Jo found herself crouching down and squeezing into the space, the dark space under the tier of seating. She dropped down on her hands and knees and followed Stephen, who was crawling along quickly. The smoke was less here and she could feel a draught of air coming from ahead. After a short while, Jo saw a small square opening in the floor and she could just make out that Stephen was on the first rungs of a ladder, disappearing down into a dark space.

'Don't' be afeared,' said Stephen: the exact words from the play she was clutching under her arm.

'I come this way all the time,' the boy called up softly, 'so as I can see the plays without paying. This is the space the actors go in to make strange sounds come from below to add to the magic of it all.'

Jo descended into what was an almost pitch black space. It was only a short way down before she was standing almost upright. Stephen took hold of her hand. Slowly, he led her to where a small chink of light indicated a half-door to the outside. Hope began to chase away the panic and, in unimaginable relief, Jo found herself emerging into the light of the afternoon, the sun now obscured by clouds of billowing smoke. Coughing and spluttering, the two stumbled away to the grassy embankment of the Thames, which was just about a safe enough distance away from the flames. Others who had escaped were gathering there, talking about how they had got out and clasping each other in happy reunion and relief at not being burnt alive.

'You've saved my life, Stephen!! You are such a brave, clever boy. How am I ever, ever going to thank you?' Jo hugged the small boy close to her.

'You are kind,' said Stephen. 'You deserved saving. Most people are not as kind as you to boys like me.'

'Thank you so much, Stephen, but come with me, I have to find someone and I have to give this,' Jo indicated the bundle of papers she was carrying, 'to someone I can trust to give it to Master William Shakespeare.'

Jo scanned the groups standing along the embankment and then her mouth fell open. Just a short distance away, a boy was running full tilt at a man standing perilously close to the edge of the embankment. She immediately recognized the man as the one in the hat with peacock feathers, the one who had given the money to the man in the attic, she also recognized the boy: it was Alex!

Jo grabbed hold of Stephen's hand and ran towards Alex just as he head-butted peacock hat with full force and sent him hurling into the muddy water of the Thames! Alex's quick foot-work, which enabled him to escape from the hands of the man's friends, was worthy of an international footballer – he swerved, dodged and doubled-backed leaving them clutching at air. He was now pounding towards Jo, who he had just spotted on the edge of his vision.

'Had to, had to do it!' Alex panted getting near to Jo, but still running. Jo and Stephen joined him as he pounded past them. The three of them ran as fast as they could, dodging through crowds and then down the small back alley that Jo had been shown by Stephen that morning. It was a good move because when they stopped, panting for breath, it was clear that no footsteps were following them.

'Did SHARP tell you to do that?' asked Jo, when they had regained their breath.

'No, no not at all. But I just felt so angry. Those men were so bad, I mean bad. They didn't care that there could have been women, children, old men, anyone, burnt alive because of their insane jealousy. And to think they have got away with it for centuries! I was livid. I do have a bit of a temper.'

'You certainly do Alex, but I think a Scottish football manager would have been well proud of your footwork and your header, not that there was a ball! The important thing is they have now been identified.'

'Yes, but we don't know their names.'

'No, we don't, but that doesn't matter. Their faces have been captured on camera.'

'Yes, you're right, let SHARP sort it out. It's not for us to do.' Alex suddenly looked down at the small boy who was with Jo. 'And who is this?'

'This is Stephen and he saved my life.'

'Pleased to meet you Stephen,' Alex solemnly shook Stephen's hand. 'We've got to be going soon, haven't we Jo?'

'Well, yes, we have to go but I need to give this,' Jo held out the bundle of papers, 'to…well, it belongs to William Shakespeare and so I think one of the actors who was in the play would be best.'

'We'd better go back then to see if they are still outside the Globe.'

'No, that could be dangerous, those men could still be looking for you. I am sure they would stop at nothing if they think you could give away their plot.'

'And… we must go, Jo. My phone is pulsing.'

'So is mine. But I can't just leave the manuscript of *The Tempest* in an alley way. You go back, Alex. And I will try and find one of the actors and give it to them.'

'No way. We go back together.'

'Excuse me,' said Stephen. who they had both temporarily forgotten about. 'I can take the play back safely to Master William Shakespeare. He is there at the fire, I saw him when we were running. He was sitting with his head in hands, his friends about him. He will be so glad that this play was saved from the fire, he loved it more than any of the others.'

Jo and Alex stood and stared at the small boy

whose wisdom was way beyond his years. With tears in her eyes Jo bent down and carefully put the manuscript in the boy's hands. 'Take the play to him Stephen and if you will, this.' Jo put her hand in her pocket and took out the poem. 'Tell him it is from Susanna'.

'I'm to say, it's from Susanna?'

'Yes, Susanna of Shottery'

'Susanna of Shottery,' the boy repeated solemnly.

Stephen turned and started to walk up the alley way.

'Stop,' called out Jo, before he got to the end. She rushed up to him, emptied all the money out of the small purse, found a small pocket in his grubby breeches and slipped the money in there – because his hands were full of *The Tempest*. Then she folded her arms around him for one last hug, kissed him on the cheek and let her tears spill over.

Jo was still crying when she and Alex, at exactly the same moment as each other, arrived back in the cleaners' room. They sorted out their clothes, and joined the crowd of teenagers in the club jumping, gyrating, twisting and thumping to the second A-M-I number of the afternoon called 'Billy No-Mates' which had a line the happy kids all knew because they joined in at the top of their voices. Suddenly Jo was smiling again, back home in the wonderful twenty-first century.

Collect the other exciting books in the Time Traveller Kids series and discover the history of famous sites in the United Kingdom

Danny's interest in history is zero, but when a mysterious boy, claiming to be from a future organisation called SHARP gets in contact with him on his mobile, Danny agrees to travel back to the Tudor period. Making friends in the long-forgotten past gets him seriously hooked on time travel, not to mention history!

Danny has become an experienced time traveller but this doesn't help him when SHARP's communication systems fail. It is the year 671, the Dark Ages and he is left stranded in the depths of winter when wolves roamed the English countryside and Danny cannot understand a word the strange people speak.

Incredibly musically gifted, Atlanta is entranced by the music of the far-into-the- future humankind. Is this what makes her agree to join the growing band of twenty first century kids who go back in time to gather information for the organisation called SHARP?

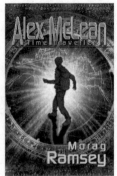

When Alex McLean is catapulted back to 1314 by a rival outfit to SHARP, his life is in serious danger. This organisation, called STRAP, do not care if he falls to his death when he joins the desperate band of Scots fighters who did the impossible and scaled the terrifying Rock on which Edinburgh Castle stands to this day.

Jo Kelly's parents, both Oxford Academics, are so busy fussing over her super bright brother, who is a chorister in the world famous Magdalen College choir, that they don't realize they are ignoring Jo. How envious they would be, if they knew that Jo is sent back in time to Oxford 1939 and that she actually meets the legendary C.S. Lewis and J.R. Tolkien.

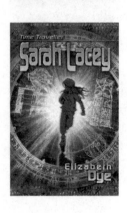

When ten-year-old Sarah accepts the challenge to travel back in time, she thought that she might meet Robin Hood. She had not bargained on joining a band of half-starved children toiling deep under ground in a south Yorkshire coalmine. She becomes a 'trapper' – a child who pulled a string to open a trap to let the trucks of coal hurtle onwards down the tunnel, that is until the mine started flooding. Sarah's life is in danger!